Rock Chick
REBORN

ROCK CHICK SERIES BOOK NINE

A ROMANCE NOVEL BY
NEW YORK TIMES BESTSELLING AUTHOR
KRISTEN ASHLEY

Rock Chick Reborn
By Kristen Ashley

This book is a work of fiction. Names, characters, places and incidents are a product of the author's imagination or are used fictitiously. Any resemblance to actual events, locales, or persons, living or dead, is coincidental.

Copyright ©2018 by Kristen Ashley

All rights reserved. In accordance with the US Copyright Act of 1976, the scanning, uploading and electronic sharing of any part of this book without permission of the publisher constitutes unlawful piracy and theft of the author's intellectual property. If you would like to use material from the book (other than for review purposes), prior written permission must be obtained by contacting the publisher at info@ kristenashley.net. Thank you for your support of the author's rights.

Cover Art and Interior Graphics: Pixel Mischief Design

ROCK CHICK REBORN

ROCK CHICK SERIES BOOK NINE

KRISTEN ASHLEY

ROCK CHICK
PRESS

This novella is dedicated to Malia Anderson, whose enthusiasm inspired me to write a story for a character who has always deserved one, but I never thought she'd get one.

This novella is also dedicated to Kristin and Brandon Harris. And I think once Kristin reads it, she'll understand why.

ACKNOWLEDGMENTS

A big thank you to all my Rock Chicks on Facebook, who were so excited about this story and helping me name Shirleen's hero, they pulled out all the stops to help me find his name.

And especially to Judy Keating, who gave me Shirleen's Moses.

It's important to note that although Gilliam Youth Services Center is a real place in Denver, Colorado, obviously I've fictionalized Moses Richardson's employment there. And here I must thank Marvy McNeese for assisting me with some insights into juvenile detention.

Last, a gratitude shout out to Liz Berry and Erika Wynne for helping me title this novella. Although we had a few good ideas, E came up with "Rebirth," which informed Shirleen's journey and became *Rock Chick Reborn*.

And as I hope you'll now discover, it was perfect.

ONE

YOUR ATTENTION

"Chicken and waffles."

"Dude, are you crazy? No chick is gonna want you making her chicken and waffles."

"I'm makin' her chicken and waffles. Everyone likes chicken and waffles."

"Yeah, and your bitch probably likes 'em too. The thing is, she'll never want *you* to know she likes 'em or that she likes *any food at all*."

At that, I stopped us all on a skid.

"If you call a woman a bitch one more time, Sniff, I'm gonna clock you back to the seventeenth century," I warned.

Me and my boys were standing in the floral section of King Soopers.

This was because Sniff and I had been warned the day before that we had to skedaddle from the house for the night because Roam was bringing over one of his bitches (and I was an adult, I could think that *and* say it) to make her dinner.

So we were shopping for said dinner and for everything else it took to raise two teenage boys, this last necessitating me being at the damned grocery store at least three times a week.

Case in point, I'd seen Roam eat an entire pack of Oreos in one sitting, open a second and hoover through a whole row.

Not an ounce of fat on the boy though.

As an aside, why was the world so unfair? A woman did that her ass would follow her into a room three weeks after she entered it.

And by the by, I mentally asked about the world being unfair a lot.

I never got an answer.

Though I shouldn't ask, because I knew the answer.

It was partly about people doing stupid shit their own damned selves, me included.

It was also that the world was just unfair.

Needless to say, raising two teenage boys meant most of the store would be in my Navigator in about an hour.

It should be noted that they weren't exactly my boys, in the sense I didn't birth either of them, and that was only obvious with one—the white one.

I was their foster mother.

They were still my boys.

Sniff, as usual, acted like he hadn't heard my warning.

He said, "Shirleen, tell him. No girl is gonna want him to make chicken and waffles for dinner, because she'll *want* him to make chicken and waffles for dinner and it'll be torture pretending she doesn't want to snarf down chicken and waffles at dinner."

I studied Sniff, eighteen and long-since having grown out of his skinny, acne-ridden early teens.

Now the boy was six foot of lean muscle, not skin and bones, and although he had a couple of acne scars, which only made his face look interesting, the excellent insurance plan I was enrolled in at work and a good dermatologist had taken care of the rest.

In other words, now he was hot.

It made me throw up a little in my mouth to think that about my boy, but the evidence was standing right in front of me wearing jeans that every mother in the country would declare illegal and a cream, short-sleeved thermal that molded to various features of his developed chest, narrowing ribs, and flat stomach.

The power that package had over teenage-girl pussy I blamed on the Hot Bunch. It was *them* that took the boys under their wing, this including physical training, but also the inescapable soaking up of general badassness. So it was *them* that had honed the bods my boys now had, including Roam's, who was a lot bulkier, taller, and a different brand of hot.

Chocolate hot.

Effective chocolate hot.

As evidenced by his serial dating.

Leading to chicken and waffles.

Sniff didn't serial date.

He serial banged.

Due to an uncomfortable conversation Hank and I had some time ago—one that put me in my bed with the vapors for two days, and one that made Hank look like he might expire from trying not to bust a gut laughing after I'd talked him into having "the talk" with the boys —Hank kept them in condoms.

They could buy their own, of course. They not only got an allowance from me for keeping their rooms clean, taking out the trash and looking after the house, they were paid interns for Nightingale Investigations.

They didn't do any of the dangerous stuff. They did stuff in the control room and stuff on the computers.

Or at least they didn't *tell* me if they did the dangerous stuff. On that I just had to trust Liam Nightingale and his band of merry badasses would do the right thing with my boys.

I was all about "don't ask, don't tell." With two teenage boys in my crib, who I loved beyond reason but who were Hot Bunch in the making, this was my new life motto and my only hold on sane.

But Hank made sure they were supplied so I didn't have to take up residence in Babies 'R' Us or factor child support into their allowances.

Thus Hank had taken me aside not two weeks ago to share that Sniff, particularly, might want to get a second job to keep him at the necessary level of prophylactics, and that I might want to buy stock in Trojan.

It was a warning.

I requested Hank engage in another conversation with both boys, roping in Roam just to make sure.

Then I took to my bed with the vapors.

"If he wants to make his girl chicken and waffles, he's gonna make his girl chicken and waffles," I decreed.

I did this even though Sniff was right, no girl was going to show she loved chicken and waffles in front of a boy.

It was ludicrous, at that age or any age. I had long since learned the only way to live in order not to do your own head in was to let it all hang out.

It was also the way of the world.

Until you learned.

Although I tried to teach my boys other practical knowledge the Hot Bunch would never be able to transfer on them—like the importance of keeping a house, laundering your clothes and being able to cook—Roam was hopeless in the kitchen.

The kid could grill a mean burger.

But other than that, frying some chicken and manning a waffle maker were the only culinary skills he'd mastered.

Sniff, on the other hand, was a savant in the kitchen. All he had to do was watch some show on Food Network, look up the recipe online, go out and get the stuff, and *boom*! There it was on a plate in front of his brother-from-another-mother and me.

He had the touch.

Good kid.

In a lot of ways.

If he'd quit trying to make up for being scrawny and pimple-faced when he was younger by tagging every piece of ass who glanced his way and would not have glanced his way two years ago.

"It's gonna be a bust," Sniff muttered.

"It's gonna be awesome," Roam returned.

"It's gonna..." I trailed off when something that felt like a finger traced lightly down the back of my neck.

For some reason, maybe instinct after being around the Hot Bunch for so long, this made me turn my attention to the rose section.

And there stood a man with an empty cart, not moving, his eyes locked on me.

And oh sweet Lord, he was beautiful.

Tall as Roam, had to be, at least six-two. Close cropped hair, close cropped beard that was thicker around his mouth, scanter but not sparse on his cheeks. Both were sprinkled very minimally with a little white.

He had wide set, big, deep-brown eyes and a beautiful brother's nose, thick and strong. Making that better, at the bridge there were a couple of creases. There were some creases in his forehead that were interesting as well, and with the white in his beard, they were the only things on his burly, wide-shouldered frame that told tale of his age.

He was just...perfect.

Even the shape of his skull sitting on the column of his neck was divine.

As I stared at him, his gaze unlocked on me to drop to my hands on the cart then it went to the boys, and a slash of white formed between his beautiful full lips, exposing strong, white teeth.

He gave us a group scan then turned to the display of roses.

"Is that brother seriously checkin' you out in front of us?" Roam asked, not happy about the possibility and not hiding it in his tone.

I turned my attention to him to see him scowling at Idris Hottie at the roses.

"No," I answered.

"He fuckin' was," Sniff rumbled, and I looked to him to see him glowering at the beautiful black man now examining a bouquet of beautiful orange roses.

"If you say fuck in front of me one more time, or *at all*, I'm knockin' you back to ancient Egypt," I promised.

Sniff ignored me, still busy frowning at the hottie at the roses.

Right, there were groceries to buy, I was hungry and I wasn't going to get to eat until they were bought, taken home, put away and Sniff and I left Roam to hopefully make his girl chicken and waffles then do nothing more than hold her hand while watching TV.

So we needed to get shit done.

"You boys are going to Walgreens," I announced.

Slowly, they both turned to me.

"Say what?" Roam asked.

"You work my nerves in a grocery store, I got things I need from the drugstore and we don't have a lot of time. I got a list," I stated, opening my raisin Artsy MM LV bag and yanking out my drugstore list, a pen and my wallet. In order for them to get the right stuff, I scrawled some words on the list before I shoved it with some cash at Sniff. "Go. Get that stuff. Come back and get me." I dug for my keys, got those and handed them to Roam. "Be good to my baby. You break it, I break you."

Sniff stared down at the list a beat then looked at me. "They got all this stuff at King Soopers."

"They do not have my nail varnish at King Soopers," I retorted.

Sniff looked back to the list then to me. "I am not buyin' nail polish called Clothing Optional."

I crossed my arms on my chest. "Tell me, boy, one day when you done notched so many marks on your bedpost you got no bedpost anymore and you want yourself an Indy..." No reaction. "A Jet..." None there either. "Roxie..." Nope. "Jules..." Surprisingly, since they were both tight with Jules and I thought they both crushed on her, that didn't hit it either. "Stella..." Hmm, nothing. "Sadie..."

His eyes flared.

So he went for the fairy princess bitches.

If they were white.

Though I'd noted my boy had a thing for the sisters.

Then again, those were the fairy princess ones too. I'd seen him with more Brandys and Gabrielles than I could shake a stick at.

"Right, you want yourself a Sadie someday, boy, you're gonna be findin' yourself buyin' a lot more than nail polish to make her happy. You think Hector blinks at nail polish?"

"Yes," he declared.

So they hadn't learned all they could learn from the Hot Bunch.

"You'd be wrong, 'cause I might not've seen him buy nail polish, but I sure as shit saw him snatching up some o.b.s and he did it like he was grabbin' a six-pack. In other words, it made no never mind to Hector Chavez he was gettin' his woman her o.b.s."

Sniff looked at Roam. "What are o.b.s?"

Roam started to look sick.

"Tampons," I educated.

Sniff started to look sick.

I could not talk about my boys having sex and the necessity of condoms.

I could sure as shit talk about this.

"You do know the menstrual cycle is a fact of life and unless there's some sad reason that makes a woman not have them, all women do," I shared. "It's entirely natural. And something you both are gonna have to deal with on a hopefully normal and healthy occasion, that is, when you settle down in a monogamous relationship with a woman you love more than your own life."

Both boys looked ready to hurl.

I heard a chuckle, and it wasn't only my eyes that went in that direction as Rose Hottie wandered into the fruit and veg section with that big bouquet of orange roses having been wrapped in pretty paper at the floral station sitting in the child seat at the top of his cart.

He had a woman.

Again, why was the world so unfair?

Sure, he looked my age and it would stand to reason that man with that face and that bod (and that deep chuckle) at his age would have a woman in his bed.

Still.

I watched him disappear around the chill case filled with Odwalla.

"Sniff can go get your nail polish. I'm stayin' with you," Roam decreed.

I turned to him. "What?"

"That guy's gonna pounce," he told me.

"He's got flowers in his cart," I told him.

"He's gonna pounce," he repeated.

"He's got flowers, boy. Means he's got a woman," I returned.

"He's. Gonna. *Pounce*."

I shut up.

Roam did not like repeating himself.

I hadn't had them long. Both boys had been fifteen when I took them on, now they were both eighteen and nearing on graduating high school.

But even back then, after all he'd been through, all he'd seen, all that had been done to him, all he'd lost, Roam had honed that edge of steel that made him, and it was the kind you never lost. It didn't matter what love you found in your life—and Jules had led both those boys to a lot of love, case in point, *me*—that kind of steel never went away.

Steel like that replaced the marrow in your bones.

It was just what happened.

When he and his bud, Park, had taken Sniff under their wing, they'd protected Sniff from a lot of what they'd endured.

And when both he and Sniff had lost Park to bad dope, Roam hadn't been able to protect Sniff from it, or protect Jules, and it was my feeling that loss, and also the fact he hadn't been able to prevent it, had changed him irrevocably.

He did not waste time.

He did not suffer fools gladly.

And he did not let anyone harm someone he loved.

He'd taken a bullet to prove that to Jules.

There were grown men who didn't have it in them to make that kind of sacrifice.

Roam had done it at the age of fifteen.

"Got no need for a man in my life, baby," I said softly. "Got the only two men I need right now, and I'm seein' to them, and only them, until they start seein' to themselves. So don't you worry, Roam. You can go to Walgreens with Sniff and I'll make sure I got enough Double Stufs to last you the week. Now you get my varnish and don't forget the lip gloss. Smoldering Eclipse."

Roam kept scowling, and this had nothing to do with him imminently having to find lip gloss in the shade of Smoldering Eclipse.

Sniff huffed out a sigh.

I endured this until eventually Sniff tagged Roam's arm and muttered, "Let's go. She won't back down. You know it. Faster we get her girlie crap, faster we can get back."

"You need us, you call," Roam ordered.

I did not inform him I was a fifty-three-year-old woman and could take care of myself.

I just rolled my eyes.

They took off.

I watched them go, thinking there was more to what I said to Roam and it wasn't the fact that man with his flowers clearly had a woman in his life.

It was that I was not going to take on another man for the rest of mine.

I'd had one and he'd changed me irrevocably, and not a bit of it was in a good way.

He hadn't left steel in the marrow of my bones.

He'd left dust.

After he was whacked, I'd gone on to make stupid decisions that affected not only me.

I had a history—an ugly one—that no man would want to take on.

And I couldn't imagine anything on this earth worse (for me) than maybe getting the attention of a beautiful man who chuckled like humor bubbled up from his soul and having to watch his face as he learned who I was and what I'd done.

Before hitting the doors, Roam stopped, turned and stared at me and years of life on the streets before I got him under my roof meant I'd have to be more badass than Lee Nightingale himself to hide anything from that boy.

But it wasn't about being badass.

It was that I didn't hide shit from my boys. They'd led lives given no reason to trust, and it had been hell teaching them they could trust me and taking that further in showing them how to find others with whom they could do the same.

I didn't blow him a kiss, send him a smile or give him a nod.

You didn't do that with Roam.

He wasn't about displays of affection.

You earned his by being real and being solid.

So I just held his gaze and looked impatient.

He turned and followed his brother out the door.

I swung my cart around and braced at the thought of facing Rose Hottie in the fruit and veg section.

He probably had a sister at home that rivaled Naomi or Halle or Taraji or Angela or Tyra.

He was nowhere to be seen.

"Lord have mercy on me," I whispered to myself as I perused apples, oranges, bananas, kiwis, spinach, cucumbers, broccoli and carrots, throwing it all in my cart even knowing I'd eat that shit myself as the boys dipped their Oreos in full-fat milk and decimated party-size bags of ranch-flavored Doritos.

Which was what I was reaching for (times three) several aisles later when I heard, "Hello."

I turned my head and looked into dark-brown eyes separated by an interestingly creased bridge of a nose in a handsome face.

Then I did something so anti-Shirleen Jackson, it was like I'd immediately formed a split personality.

I bolted.

Shit, Roam was right.

No man called attention to himself by greeting some woman reaching for Doritos.

Unless he wanted to pounce.

Goddamn!

I was halfway through the next aisle when I realized I hadn't nabbed the cheddar cheese Ruffles for Roam, or the Pringles smorgasbord for both of them. So I motored down the aisle, swung wide to the next one, motored down that one, caught Rose Hottie studying the water selection (which, with those shoulders, he probably drank while lifting weights) in the aisle that stood between me and the boys' Pringles.

I boogied as fast as my Louboutin Konstantina pompom flats would take me (which was fast, and that was good since I had to go fast, but it was bad since I wished being in that man's presence I'd been wearing a pair of heels, specifically my new Alexander Wang black Rina beaded slingbacks, though I wasn't sure they went with my LV, still they were hot).

I circled back into the snack aisle and got the Pringles, Ruffles and Chex Mix on the trot, making sure to nab the cheesy crackers both boys loved (times four).

Rose Hottie was out of the water and soda aisle, thankfully, as I had stocking up to do there. But as I hit the cleaning supplies section, he was perusing fabric softener.

I also needed fabric softener.

His head came around.

So I did a U-ey with my cart and hightailed my ass out of there, liberally (as usual) stocking up on paper towels (sorry environment, but I had two teenage boys, they didn't understand global warming or the concept of reusable rags, no matter how much I drilled that shit in their heads) and Charmin.

I circled back when the coast was clear for fabric softener.

It happened in the three-aisle freezer section.

I had to get tater tots and crinkle cuts. Not to mention a hefty supply of DiGiornos. Roam might starve to death if he couldn't bake a frozen pizza when I was out, and I was a Rock Chick so I was out a lot. I also had two teenage boys who obsessively maintained social lives and their badass training so they weren't home all that much, but when they got home, they were hungry. The entire freezer in the garage was taken up with DiGiornos and we were running low.

But Rose Hottie was now on a mission. His fine black ass (and yes, I'd caught a glimpse and yes, it almost sent me into vapors) had speeded up and every time he saw me, him and his cart made a beeline to me.

I lost him when I was doing my usual Hail Mary with the frozen peas (I'd eat all those too), and as I trucked out of the frozen food section and loaded up with milk and creamer, as well as hit the cheese aisle, he was gone.

Bad.

Good.

Bad.

No, good.

But it felt bad.

Since it felt bad, it was not the boys, but me who scored an entire birthday cake (but in the end the boys would eat most of it) and I thought of my girl, Daisy, and her lover man, Marcus. I also thought of Indy and how deeply she was adored by Lee. And Jet, who was practically worshipped by Eddie. And then there was Roxie, who was beloved to Hank. Jules and Vance. Ava and Luke. Stella and Mace. Sadie and Hector. Ally and Ren. Tod and Stevie. Ralphie and Buddy. Tex and Nancy.

I was staring at the bagels and fresh rolls in the bakery section, close to tears...

Me.

Shirleen Jackson.

Widow of the lowdown, good-for-nothin' Leon Jackson.

Ex-drug dealer.

I was tough.

I'd lived through hell.

And there I was, near tears in the bakery section of King Soopers.

Because I wanted a badass.

I wanted to be adored, beloved, worshipped by a good man who saw nothing but good in me.

I'd wanted that for as long as I could remember.

And it wasn't going to happen.

Not for me.

Never for me.

Because life was unfair.

But the worst of it was...

I'd made it that way.

CRASH!

I jumped back as my cart slammed into the bagel display, toilet paper packs and Bounty wobbling, full-fat milk glugging, chips rustling, boxes of DiGiornos nearly toppling, cart ending up jammed against the shelves under the bagels, caged there by another cart that was nearly as full as mine.

I turned my head to see Rose Hottie, hands still on the cart that had plowed into my own.

"Now that I have your attention."

Oo...

Wee.

His voice was honey.

Warm, sweet, deep, delicious honey.

Hell's fire.

"Uh..." I forced out.

"I'm Moses," he declared.

Oh Lord.

Good name.

Great name.

Goddamn.

"Um..." I mumbled.

"Moses Richardson."

I got kinda lost in watching his lips moving.

They moved again.

"Now's the time you tell me your name," he ordered.

My eyes lifted to his.

Bad idea.

He had fabulous eyes. Open, amused and curious.

"I'm grocery shopping," I shared.

His eyes turned more amused.

"Is that your name?" he asked.

"No."

"I hadn't really missed that," he told me, tipping his head to my cart.

I decided not to say anything more.

He didn't take the hint and unjack my cart from the bakery display.

He gave my cart a thorough examination before looking again at me and inquiring, "Those your boys?"

"Uh...what?"

"At the entrance. Those boys you were with. Ten frozen pizzas in your cart. They yours?"

"Yep."

Expressive eyebrows went up.

"Both of them?" he pushed.

"Yep," I pushed out.

"You got a brother?" he asked.

"As in the sibling kind?" I asked back.

"No," he answered.

"No," I answered.

"Hard to make that white one with a brother," he decreed.

"Uh...yeah," I agreed.

"Adopted?" he kept at me.

"Foster," I shared.

That's when it happened.

We were in the bakery section and it felt like the ovens had all been dialed up, doors open, warming the place with bakery-oven goodness.

"You're a foster momma?" he queried softly.

"Just…just them."

"How long they been with you?"

"Three years."

"So they're yours," he pressed.

My chin lifted half an inch. "They're mine."

More warmth, not from the ovens, coming direct from him.

Moses Richardson.

Damn.

"What's your name?" he asked.

It was time to pull my shit together.

I tried to unwedge my cart, muttering, "I gotta go."

He shoved my cart in farther, damaging the bagged, cardboard trays of Hawaiian rolls on the shelves under the bagels.

I looked back to him.

"They'll like me," he announced.

I stared.

Was this brother seriously jumping that far ahead?

"Because I like you," he explained.

"You don't know me," I pointed out.

"Yeah I do."

That felt nice.

I still shook my head.

For his sake.

And mine.

"You don't and you won't."

"I do and I will."

It was time to snap back to Shirleen.

"Listen, my man, you need to move your cart. I got shit to do. My boys'll be back soon and Roam's got a girl comin' over tonight, and we gotta get him set up before Sniff and I hit Jerusalem."

He looked impressed. "Combo platter?"

You were either vegetarian or not from Denver if you didn't get the combo (or meat) platter at Jerusalem.

"Absolutely."

More warmth and then, "Roam?"

"The black one."

"I mean the name," he clarified.

"Street name. Same with Sniff."

Another brow lift. "You let them go by their street names?"

"There were battles to wage when they hit my crib, that wasn't one of them."

"I can imagine," he murmured.

I took him in. Dark-wash jeans. Pressed button-down. Discreet, but attractive, curb-chained gold bracelet peeking from his cuff. Good boots.

He had no fucking clue.

"No, you can't," I snapped.

His eyes stared right into mine.

"Work at Gilliam. Corrections officer. I can."

Gilliam.

Gilliam Youth Services Center.

Denver juvie.

Well...shit.

"Three years, those boys. You took them in at what, sixteen? Seventeen? There are about negative two hundred good foster mommas in Denver who'd take in boys that age, that size, with street names and a hundred years they never should have lived on their faces. But then there was you," he decreed.

I started to feel goose bumps forming all over my skin.

"They were fifteen," I said quietly.

"Same shit, different age," he replied.

He was so right about that.

"Listen, Moses—"

"I want to take you to dinner."

I snapped my mouth shut.

"You're the most beautiful sister I've seen in ten years, and I thought that before I knew what you were to those boys," he went on.

Oh Lord.

That felt *nice*.

"I—"

"Don't say no," he whispered.

I swallowed.

"I got two teenage daughters, which might not be good with those two boys, but we'll tackle that when we face it," he kept at me. "And I got an ex-wife who didn't make it easy in the beginning, but we got a flow now and we been ridin' that for seven years, divorced for eleven, so we got it down and she's not a problem. You're not wearing a ring, you got an ex?"

"My man's dead."

"I'm sorry," he said gently.

"I'm not," I returned.

At that, he studied me.

And as it seemed was his way, he threw it right out there.

"Didn't do you right?" he asked.

"We're not talking about this," I told him.

He gave one nod of that perfectly-formed skull. "Right. Good call. We'll talk about it over dinner."

I had to escape this.

Now.

For him.

And me.

"Listen, Moses—"

"Please God, woman, don't say no."

I shut my mouth again.

I opened it to warn, "Trust me, you do not want to take this on."

He shook his head at that. "I do."

"You really don't."

"I absolutely do."

It was then, I looked right into his eyes.

"You absolutely do not."

He was not deterred.

Damn it.

"How about you let me decide that."

"How about you move your cart so I can keep on keepin' on."

His head tipped to the side. "You not into me?"

Was he seriously living in that body, having that face, that voice, those crinkles on his nose and that manner and asking that shit?

I decided a question that stupid wasn't worthy of an answer.

Amusement lit his eyes again. "You're into me."

"I got a job herding badasses, and I got two badasses hoovering through Oreos and Doritos at my house. I don't need another badass on my hands."

He bent into his forearms on the bar of his cart, making his shoulders ripple under his shirt that tightened on them, which made something ripple in one specific part of me, him doing this like we were going to crack open a bottle of wine and stay awhile in the bakery section as he asked, "What's your job that you herd badasses?"

I started jimmying my cart to try to disengage it, muttering, "We're not doin' this."

"Stop," he demanded.

I looked at him again.

"Move," I demanded.

He did.

He moved from the handle of his cart toward me, one arm behind his back.

I froze.

He pulled out his wallet.

"Got a pen?" he asked.

"Uh…" I mumbled because he was close and he smelled good.

Like…

Real good.

He stopped even closer. So close, I had to tip my head to look into those brown eyes.

"Baby, I asked, you got a pen in that classy bag of yours?" he murmured.

After Leon got whacked, I decided in my life I was not ever doing anything I didn't want to do.

And one could not say that I didn't want to look down to my bag, open it, pull out a pen and hand it to Moses Richardson.

What one could say, that one being *me*, was that I had no control over my actions.

Him that close, looking that good, smelling that amazing, if he asked me if I had a honey-baked ham in my bag, I would have rushed to the deli, grabbed one, sprinted back, shoved it in my LV (no matter that broke all the laws of my universe) so I could pull it out and hand it to him.

In other words, I gave him my pen.

He wrote on a white card on the back of his wallet then he returned his wallet to his jeans, offering the pen and card to me.

"My card. My cell number on the back. And your call. You think on it, you want dinner, you call me. Then you buy a nice dress. Because no way, when you call me, I'm not doin' it up right."

Slowly, my hand lifted and took the card and pen.

He didn't let it go.

At first.

"What's your name?" he whispered.

"Shirleen," I whispered back, staring in those eyes.

Those eyes warmed and that warmth warmed me.

Straight to my bones.

Where I'd been cold a really, *really* long time.

"It was nice to meet you, Shirleen," he said softly.

He let go of the card only to stroll the three feet in order drop his hand to the roses that I now saw had a receipt stapled to the paper so

I could walk right out with them. He came back and rested them on my LV in the child seat.

After he pulled that class move, I watched him go back to the handle of his cart.

He pulled his cart from mine, and looking over his shoulder to shoot me a white smile, he walked away.

TWO

SO FAR AWAY

"Jesus, what's all this shit?"

I saw a strong, long-fingered, veined hand reach toward my pack of sorbet wet erase markers and did the only thing I could do.

I reached out, slapped it sharply and shot from my chair to my feet behind my desk in the reception area of Nightingale Investigations to face off against Luke Stark.

I also snapped, "Don't touch anything! I'm getting organized!"

Luke stood across the desk from me wearing a black T-shirt, blue jeans and a shocked expression on his badass face.

He'd recently given up on his legendary Fu Manchu mustache and had grown in a full, black beard.

I missed the Fu Manchu. There was exactly one man on the planet who could pull it off—Luke—but *he could pull it off*.

Saying that, the man was fine, so the beard far from sucked.

"You're getting what?" he asked.

"Organized," I clipped.

"What?" he repeated.

"*Organized*," I bit out impatiently.

I mean, *sheesh*.

I *was* the office manager at the private investigations firm where he worked.

Granted, I didn't file. And I generally didn't organize. I mostly helped Lee dodge anything that might chain him to his desk, like putting off appointments, or taking them in his stead, or paying bills, or sending invoices or cutting paychecks. But, except for the last (which was mostly automated), I did it all when the spirit moved me (for instance when my nails didn't need a new coat or when the latest *Us Weekly* hadn't been released).

Lee was cool I rolled that way.

Still, everyone could be better organized.

Including me.

And no, I was not using purchasing hundreds of dollars of planner shit as a way to escape the fact it had been a week since I'd met Moses Richardson at King Soopers, and I could not call him no matter how weak I wanted to be (and in that weakness, call him immediately).

And no, I would not be using organizing the shit out of my life and every life that touched my life, including every member of the Hot Bunch, as a way to continue to escape that.

Even though I was oh so totally doing that.

Bottom line, Luke should be happy.

Not giving me shit.

He looked down at the healthy (okay, ridiculously out of hand) display of planner and planner accoutrement littering the entirety of the top of my large desk, and then he looked back at me.

"With purple markers, stickers and Post-its with flowers on them?" he queried.

"I'm creating a system," I shared as the front door opened.

I didn't look to it when Luke asked, "A system that includes purple markers and stickers?"

What was he not understanding about this?

"Yes. It's all about color coordination, creativity and visual stimulation."

"Jesus, what's all this shit?" Vance Crowe asked, eyes down to my desk, body coming to stand on one side of Luke.

Hector Chavez appeared on Luke's other side.

"Fuck," Hector muttered, also staring at the desk.

Most women, facing off with that kind of eye candy in close proximity, would pass out.

Yes, these men were that hot.

Seriously.

No female brain could stay conscious with Luke Stark, Vance Crowe and Hector Chavez two feet away from them.

Fortunately, I'd grown immune to it.

(That was a lie, but I'd become accustomed to it.)

Vance, quicker on the move than his bros, probably due to his history as an ex-con, reached out and nabbed my pack of gem-tone markers.

He then waved them in the air. "I'm pretty sure Lee wrote in the employee handbook that there are no pink markers allowed on the premises."

"That's not pink," I shared. "It's fuchsia." I reached out to the sorbet pack and tapped it with my nail (coated in Clothing Optional of course). "*This* one has the pink."

Seeing as Vance was taking my attention, I didn't clock Hector picking up a sheet of stickers.

"You got somethin' wrong with your hand?" he asked.

"No," I answered.

"Then why you got stickers that say 'trash day,' 'treat yo'self,' 'laundry time,' and 'but first, coffee' when you can write that shit out yourself?"

"Because they have a cute font and cute little pictures," I told him as the door to the inner sanctum opened. "And they're *stickers*. Everyone likes *stickers*."

"Little kids like stickers," Vance pointed out.

He'd know. He was in the process of making an army of them with Jules.

"I'm becoming one with my inner child," I informed him snottily.

"So you're organizing *your* life, you're not using stickers and purple markers to organize the men," Luke declared, like he'd *just about* allow this but only under some duress.

"I'm organizing all you all's asses too," I shared and finished, "With purple markers. Though *you're* purple, as in grape sorbet," I told Luke. "Vance is teal. And Hector is amethyst."

"Shit," Hector muttered.

"Holy fuck," Mace muttered, rounding the end of my desk with Lee, eyes aimed down, and stopping there.

When Lee came to a halt with Mace, his brows hiked high. "What's all this shit?"

Thank God I no longer carried a switchblade.

"I'm *organizing!*" I nearly shouted.

Lee reached out and tagged the pack of handy, glittery, metallic elastic bands I bought to keep my planner closed, say, when I threw it in my purse or in my car.

"Did you buy this shit on the business account?" he asked.

"Some of it," I answered.

Lee's brows sunk low and most people, men or women, would lose control of their bladder at that look.

I was accustomed to it.

"You bought stickers with mushrooms on them on the NI dime?" Mace asked, waving my autumn stickers.

"Those are for around Thanksgiving time," I shared as the door to the inner sanctum opened again.

"And this is?" Hector asked, and I looked to him to see him brandishing a laminated picture that had a pink peppermint house with a snowflake on the door, a curlicue pine tree next to it fashioned in white and glitter, and swirls and snowflakes in the air all around against a blue background with my name in pink on it.

"That's my Christmas cover," I explained. "I have one for Thanksgiving, Easter, the Fourth of July and one for when I'm wearing blacks and silvers, instead of browns and golds."

"You change the cover of your planner with your outfit?" Vance asked.

"And the season," I answered.

"That go on the business account too?" Lee asked.

I swung to him. "Hell no."

Though the Thanksgiving, Easter, Fourth of July and etcetera stickers went on it because they had ones that said To Do.

"*Ohmigod! Dope! You got planner stickers!*" Brody, the Nightingale Investigations computer guru (meaning nerd, alternately meaning hacker, but mostly it was nerd) shrieked (see? nerd). He dashed around the desk to stand by me, his hand snaking out to grab the entire sheet that had stickers that said, Jammin' on my planner. He looked at me with bright shining in his eyes that was undimmed through his Buddy Holly glasses. "Can I have a sheet of these?"

Since those were on the NI dime too, I stated magnanimously, "Knock yourself out."

"Whoa!" Brody yelled, looking back down to my desk. "Where'd you get these ones that say 'don't be a dick' and 'fuck this'? I gotta get some of those."

I decided not to meet any eyes as I replied, "Take one. I bought five."

"Yee ha!" he cried, snatching it up.

"Who's Moses Richardson?"

My heart clean stopped in my chest, but my eyes moved to Hector.

They did this slowly, but they moved.

He was holding Moses's business card.

Stupid me, I'd upended most of my purse on my desk in my quest to get organized.

And since I was carrying around Moses's card like a personal talisman, it had fallen out.

Then again, none of the men had ever shown the least interest in what was on my desk.

And then again to that, it was rare anything was on my desk but a bottle of nail varnish and/or acetone.

Hector's attention was on the card.

"Director of Juvenile Probation." He looked at me. "You got a problem with the boys?"

"No," I pushed out.

"There's a number on the back," Brody informed Hector helpfully.

Hector flipped the card.

Luke turned his head to look at it. Vance leaned in to look across Luke at it. Mace was also looking at it even if, from his position, he couldn't see it. Though he had badass vision, so maybe he could see it, what did I know? I was a little badass but not like them.

Lee was watching me.

"Can you all move along?" I asked as a demand. "I've got a plan to organize your mission for tonight with peach sorbet being tactical and lime sorbet being surveillance."

Luke looked to me. "You seein' a juvie officer, Shirleen?"

Most of the time, considering some of the stuff they did was vaguely illegal and not-so-vaguely unsafe, I thought it was great they were all highly intelligent and uncannily perceptive.

This was not one of those times.

"We met. He asked me out. I said no. He gave me his card should I rethink. The end," I told him.

Luke looked to Lee.

Mace looked to Vance.

Hector looked back down at the card.

Brody looked at me. "Why'd you say no?"

"Have I ever struck you as a woman who shares her personal life?" I asked.

"I was over at your house watching *Tarzan* two weeks ago and you pulled out your family albums," Brody reminded me. "All twelve of them."

Damn.

"I was drunk," I lied.

"You were not." He called me on it.

"Alexander Skarsgård got me to feelin' sentimental," I snapped.

"That, from you, I can believe," Vance muttered.

I swept a hand above my desk. "Does it look like I don't have things to do? Once I color code your mission tonight, I have a year's worth of holiday stickers to stick into my planner, and that shit includes Flag Day and cyber Monday and Palm Sunday, so it's gonna be in*tense*. In other words, I got shit *to do*."

"Why'd you say no?" Lee asked.

Oh no.

This question did not bode well.

And the intent way he was examining my face boded even worse.

"This really isn't your business," I replied quietly.

Lee held my eyes.

But he'd broken the seal.

"You not into him?" Luke asked.

I turned my attention to Luke. "I already got a full life, don't need anything making it fuller."

"You're into him," Luke whispered.

Shit.

"There's full, Shirleen, then there's full," Vance noted.

"Are we really standing around my desk talking about my love life?" I demanded.

"No," Lee stated shortly. "We're standin' around it talking about the fact you don't have one."

"And how's that your business?" I queried sharply.

Every single man, including nerdy Brody, leaned back from my desk in badass affront (the badass part not including Brody).

Okay, I had to give them that since I meddled in almost all of theirs (save Brody, who didn't have one (yet) and Lee, considering I wasn't around when he and Indy hooked up—okay, all of theirs).

"This isn't the same," I stated.

"Yeah, you're right. This isn't the same as you helpin' Ava get dressed up to go out on a date with another guy when she was sleepin' in my bed," Luke rumbled.

Oh Lordy.

"That wasn't *a date*," I reminded him. "It was a thank-you dinner. And anyway, Ava was the first Rock Chick I was in charge of. I didn't have a lot of experience."

This was now years ago, the woman was wearing his ring, and he still did not look happy this event occurred.

Damn, I *told* that girl it was a bad idea. Did she listen to me? Noooooo. She went. On a thank-you dinner that seemed a lot like a date with a hot guy the man whose bed she was sleeping in didn't like all that much, primarily because he'd asked the woman who was sleeping in his bed out to a thank-you dinner that was really a date.

And now she was *still* sleeping in Luke's bed, doing it with a ring on it, and was she paying for that shit *she* pulled?

Noooooo.

She was getting the business.

Regular.

While I'd named my vibrator Eustace because he knew me better than any man on earth.

And I was getting Ava's man all up in *my* business.

"And that guy she went out on a date with is who my sister is now *livin'* with," Lee put in.

Hmm.

I shut up.

"You went with Sadie when she reported her rape."

After Hector spoke, I pulled my lips in and looked at him.

"You're a member of this family, Shirleen," he said quietly. "Once you're in, there's no way out. What I'm thinkin' you might not get with this is," he flapped Moses's card in front of himself, "that's a good thing."

"He crashed his cart into mine at King Soopers," I blurted.

Me!

Shirleen Jackson.

Blurting!

To badasses!!!

"Deliberately?" Mace growled.

Oh boy.

Short-fuse Mace.

He was getting it regular too, from his woman Stella, so his fuse should be less short.

But he, like all the Hot Bunch boys, was of the Roam variety.

You didn't fuck with someone he loved.

"I'd been kinda, um…running away from him all through the frozen food section," I explained.

Vance's head dropped *and* turned to the side.

I still saw his shit-eating grin.

And his body shaking with silent laughter.

What I said didn't make Mace much happier.

"So you clearly didn't want his attention, he shoulda took the hint and backed the fuck off."

All of the men dropped their heads and looked to the side at that.

"Yeah, and how'd that work for you when you so delicately pursued Stella after she told you repeatedly you guys were over?" I asked.

Mace's jaw went hard.

"Unh-hunh," I said on a head snap.

Lee came back to the conversation before I could carry on about how he'd not backed off from Indy when she'd tried to make him do so (and Vance had not done that with Jules, or Luke from Ava, and so on). "So you're into him, and he's chasing you through the frozen food section. Why'd you say no?"

"He's attractive, but not my type."

"What's your type?" Vance asked curiously.

"Not him."

Brody piped up. "Alexander Skarsgård. Gerard Butler. Dwayne Johnson. Idris Elba—"

His mouth was still open when I turned and ordered, "Shut up, Brody."

His mouth closed.

I was glaring at him and mentally deciding no more Brody-Shirleen Movie Nights (at least for a month, what could I say, Brody and I had similar cinematic leanings) when Luke declared, "We're on mission in an hour."

"Yeah, and it's not color coded yet," I put in.

Luke gave me a blank look.

Vance shook his head.

The rest of the men started to move away.

"My card," I snapped at Hector, who still had Moses's card.

Hector turned back, mouth open.

Vance's mouth opened.

Mace's mouth opened.

I didn't look, but I was sure Brody's mouth opened.

Luke's mouth thinned.

But it was Lee who spoke.

"Give her back the card, Hector."

Hector set it on my desk, his liquid black gaze to me before it shifted to Lee.

I didn't touch it or say another word as all the men moved through the door to the inner sanctum.

Only then did I snatch it up and clip it with one of my (four) new magnetic paper clips to the week of Christmas, which was nine months away.

Because I had a feeling Moses Richardson was like Christmas when it was April.

Joy and goodness and dreams coming true...
But still...
So far away.

Lee Nightingale

Twenty-four hours later...

Lee walked into the control room, asking, "What we got?"

Luke shifted away from the desk Hector and Mace were also standing at to expose Vance in a chair, rolling over from the other desk in the room to the one Monty was sitting behind with his laptop in front of him.

Monty looked up from the laptop and didn't fuck around with laying it out.

"Moses James Richardson. Fifty-one years of age. Army, honorable discharge. Distinguished Service Cross recipient." His eyes locked on Lee's. "Kuwait. Sierra Leone. Bosnia. Kuwait. Somalia. Bosnia."

"Holy fuck," Lee whispered.

"His boots got dusty," Monty replied.

"Shit yeah," Lee replied, impressed.

That kind of résumé meant his unit was elite.

Monty looked back to the laptop. "Married seven years. Divorce acrimonious, but since then they've straightened shit out and his ex is remarried. Two daughters, one seventeen, one fifteen. Both honor roll. Oldest drill team. Youngest, sophomore class president."

"How'd he get into juvie work?" Lee asked.

"Far's I can see from his interview notes, he had a cousin. His uncle was a good man, kid just had a tendency to go off the rails. Kid was younger than him, but Richardson took him under his wing. They were tight, helped keep him on the straight and narrow as best he could. While Richardson was occupied with earning his Distinguished Service Cross, the cousin got into some trouble that bought him being tried as an adult at seventeen and hitting the big house for a dime. After Richardson got out of the Army, used the GI Bill to get his degree, went into the Academy, became a beat cop, made detective. But eventually he moved over. Did his time as a juvenile corrections officer, now he oversees that outfit. What we got, he's still very hands on with the kids in a way it's not a job, it's a mission."

Monty turned the laptop around and on it was the photo panel of a Facebook page album entitled "Me and my dad."

His youngest daughter was pretty.

Her dad was built.

And the man was good-looking.

"So no red flags," Lee noted, starting to look at Monty, but Luke grunting switched his attention.

It was Monty who spoke.

"He undoubtedly knew Park and probably knew Roam. Which means he might know Shirleen."

Lee felt his neck get tight. "Say again."

"Both Park and Roam went through Gilliam, Lee," Monty shared. "Richardson was there when they were there. Park was there more often than Roam. Roam only hit juvie once, Park was there repeatedly."

"So how's he gonna know Shirleen?" Lee asked.

"It wasn't exactly off radar how Jules and King's Shelter finagled that placement, two teenage street kids placed in foster care with an ex-drug dealer who had not gone through the program. This right after a social worker was shot twice trying to protect one of those kids. It caused some ripples. It isn't a stretch this guy, working in the system as long as he has for the reasons he quit being a cop and became a JCO, heard that word."

"You think he has some problem with her?" Lee pushed.

"I think if there's anyone who knows the difference between people who fuck up their lives with no intention to change them and people who made stupid decisions in their lives, and worked their asses off and or put them on the line to get their shit sorted or get clean, and admires it, it's this guy," Monty answered.

"But we can't know that," Luke growled.

Monty shook his head but did it in agreement. "We can't know that."

"So before we go all matchmaker, we feel this guy out," Luke declared.

Lee turned to Luke. "Absolutely."

"I want on him for a day or two," Vance, their best tracker, said. "And I want in his house."

None of them were slouches on that front, but Vance was also best with a B&E.

"Do it," Lee obliged.

"You do the house, I'll do the follow," Mace said.

"We gotta pass off on the follow, seein' as we're all famous now. This guy, he might tag a tail," Hector reminded them. "So we gotta pass off, especially if he tags one of us."

"You get made, you share. Means we all gotta back off," Lee ordered. "Thanks to those fuckin' newspaper articles and books, one and one will make two, he sees more than one *Hot Bunch* guy."

There were a variety of lip curls to share how they all felt about that, none of them amused in the least.

Hector nodded.

Lee looked to Monty. "He cheat on his wife? She cheat on him? What went down?"

"Court records stated irreconcilable differences. No claims of infidelity recorded. He fought for more visitation with his girls, she fought against it. I can't know why she did that, but he got it and both girls went closed chambers with the judge in order to ask for more time with their dad. That shit hit him hard financially, lotta time in court, lotta legal fees, but he didn't back down. By the time he won split visitation, the girls were eight and ten. So they'd been battling it out for four years."

"Thought dual visitation was the standard now," Vance remarked.

Monty shook his head. "She played the cop and corrections officer card. How he's never home. How his job was dangerous. How they needed limited exposure to that. She had a good attorney. Chewed him up. He got smart. Switched firms. Got himself a shark. He also got in debt." Monty turned back to Lee. "Worked his ass off, but he got outta that debt and managed to keep up his court ordered deposits into the girls' college accounts, not to mention child support, through it all. But he lived tight, way tight, through the fight and after it. Just not when he had those girls."

"Solid guy," Lee whispered.

"On file, solid as they get," Monty agreed.

"I wanna know what went down with that divorce and why she went all out to keep his girls from him," Lee told the room at large.

"I'll get Brody on that," Luke told him. "We might have to get creative."

"Do it."

Luke nodded.

Monty lifted up a hand and scratched the back of his neck as he asked, "Any of us got a problem with this dude rammin' into her grocery cart?"

Monty had been briefed.

"No," Hector said immediately.

"No," Vance said with him.

"No," Luke said half a second after them.

Mace paused and grinned at Lee before he said, "No."

Lee looked right at Monty.

"No."

"I'd worry about this modern-day Neanderthal crap if your women weren't as totally devoted to you as they are," Monty muttered, dropping his hand.

"A woman is worth it—" Luke started.
"You gotta be willing to go all in," Mace went on.
"And Shirleen's worth it," Lee finished.
It took a beat.
But after that beat…
Monty smiled.

THREE

SLICE OF HEAVEN

Lee Nightingale

Seventy-two hours later...

LEE WAS LEANING against his company Explorer, boots crossed at the ankles, arms crossed on his chest, head turned to the side, watching the man walk across the parking lot toward him.

Also noting he was more impressive in person.

For his part, Moses Richardson had not missed he had company waiting for him at the SUV parked next to his truck. The man didn't take his eyes off Lee the entire journey from front door to vehicles.

When he arrived, he also didn't keep his distance.

He got close before he stopped between the two cars, planted his legs and crossed his own arms on his chest.

Richardson started it.

And he did it with a grin on his lips.

"Gotta admit, didn't expect this visit. But I'm thinkin' it means good things."

In other words, introductions were unnecessary.

"If you're thinking Shirleen set us on you to make sure you're good enough for her, you'd be wrong. She has no idea," Lee replied.

The grin vanished.

"So obviously we gotta sort that shit," Lee continued. "But seein' as I got no idea how to do that, I'm afraid I gotta tell you it's gonna be necessary to get my wife involved, which probably means all the Rock Chicks, so this meeting is multi-purpose, and the one I'm talkin' about now means you best brace."

"Outside of tellin' my daughters they can't read those books until they're forty-five, even though they both really want to, I know *who* you're talking about. I just don't know *what* you're talking about with any of this, man."

"Shirleen is never going to call you," Lee announced.

Richardson didn't hide looking disappointed, but he nodded, not taking his eyes from Lee. "So she's not gonna do that, why are you here? And I'll repeat, what are you talking about?"

"I'm making a reservation at Barolo Grill," Lee told him. "She'll think she's having dinner with the Rock Chicks. But she'll be having dinner with you."

Richardson's brows shot up but he didn't say anything.

"Once that happens," Lee went on, "it'll be up to you to get in there."

"If she doesn't want—" Richardson started.

Lee pushed away from his truck, turned to fully face the man, put his hands on his hips and said quietly, "She wants. She's still not gonna call you."

"And you're setting her up because…?" Richardson prompted.

"Because you're a good man and she's a good woman and it's time she had some happy in her life."

His eyes narrowed. "She's not happy?"

Good point to hone in on.

Lee approved.

"I'm talking about the kind we're hopin' *you* can give her, not her boys givin' her, not the Rock Chicks givin' her, not her bossin' around my men givin' her. I think you get me."

"I get you. I'm still not sure why we're standing here having this conversation."

"You know who she is, don't you," Lee stated.

Richardson drew a visible breath in through his nose before he shared, "Wasn't sure. Kid looked a lot different when I had him at Gilliam. It's been a while and he grew up and good since he was thirteen. And we don't allow street names. But after she told me she was a foster parent and when she gave me her name, yeah, I knew who she was and I knew who her boy was."

Lee studied him closely. "Okay, so you know who she is, do you know who she *was?*"

Richardson didn't break eye contact. "If you mean do I know she's Leon Jackson's widow and that her and Darius Tucker took over the kingdom when the king was dead, yeah, I know that too."

"And you still gave her your number."

"She's out of the game and so is her nephew. They're both on board with you. So yeah, I gave her my number and straight up, it's been a bummer she hasn't used it."

Lee said nothing to that.

Richardson tipped his head to the side, beginning to look impatient.

"Is this a setup for a setup or is this a test, you feelin' me out?" he asked.

"Both," Lee answered.

That got him a look that said the man was getting pissed.

"I'm way too old for this kinda shit," Richardson told him.

Yeah, he was getting pissed.

"And I'm way too fuckin' protective to let anyone near Shirleen that might hurt her in any way, and I'm just one of many who would not be pleased she even got bruised, much less broken," Lee shot back.

"Part of the bein' too old shit is being any part of a setup that blindsides some woman who doesn't really wanna have dinner with me," Richardson returned.

"She doesn't want to have dinner with you because she thinks when you learn about her history, you won't want her."

Richardson shut his mouth so fast, his chin dipping sharply back into his neck, it was clear he hadn't thought of that.

"She didn't lose your number, man, to the point she clipped it to Christmas in her planner," Lee shared, with this in the cards, not having a problem invading Shirleen's space to see where she was at with Moses Richardson.

Christmas.

He didn't have to be a private investigator to know what that said about where she was at.

"Shit," Richardson whispered.

He knew where she was at too.

"Yeah," Lee agreed. "Now she's not gonna call you, but she wants to call you. And I want her to have what she wants. I want her to find her piece of happiness. Those boys are gonna graduate next month and they're gonna start to get on with their lives, and they will never lose her. You need to understand that. They will not ever lose her. But they're the kind of boys that will get on with their lives and how they'll do that, big parts of her life she'll be alone, and my guess from all this, she's hung up on her past so she won't ever do anything about it."

Richardson just stared at him.

"And I'll admit," Lee carried on, "in order not to give you a call to try it out with you, and in order not to think about the fact those boys're gonna be moving on soon, she's bought herself a bunch of shit to organize herself, the office, and my men. My marker is black, but my man Mace's marker is strawberry fuckin' sorbet, what she calls it, but it's pink. And to say he's not a big fan of that is an understatement. He's not even a fan of being color coded with a marker at all. But definitely not pink. And I hit my desk last night to see 'date night' stickers all over it, givin' me the not subtle hint I need to look after my woman, and my man Luke had a note in his cubby that had a sticker on it that said 'grocery shopping' with a list Shirleen got from his wife. Now if we don't turn her mind to something else, I can't even begin to guess what shit is going to go down at the office."

"So this whole thing is self-serving," Richardson noted, his lips twitching.

"Shit yeah," Lee replied.

The lip twitch stopped.

"I don't care what she was," Richardson said quietly. "What she did, she has to make her peace with herself and God. What she is now is the only thing that interests me, and I saw her handle those boys. I know she cleaned up her life. I know it takes courage to do that. Turning your back on that kind of life isn't easy, and it isn't safe, and she did it. So I want to get to know her for more than the fact she's a beautiful woman. But I don't have crystal ball, Nightingale. I don't know how this is going to turn out. I just know I won't hurt her. Now if we don't spark..." He let that trail off and lifted his shoulders.

Lee called him on that. "You know you're gonna spark or you wouldn't have given her your card."

Richardson didn't reply.

Lee nodded. "You pick the night. I'll get the reservation. Indy, my wife, will get her there."

At that, Richardson studied Lee closely. "Are you sure this is a good idea?"

Lee shook his head. "Absolutely not. The only thing I know is that I watched Shirleen Jackson stand beside women as they fought their way through a load of shit to get to the other side and find their happy. It's her turn. That might not be you, man, but I want it to be somebody and she needs to break the seal. Leon put her through hell. She paid her penance. It's time she found her slice of heaven."

"Jesus, you really care about her," Richardson murmured.

"There's a long line of those and I'm not even at the front," Lee replied.

"Make the reservation. Tuesday."

At that, Lee smiled.

"How deep was the dive?" Richardson asked.

Lee stopped smiling.

"You're Lee Nightingale," Richardson went on. "And you're here trying to convince me to go on a mostly blind date with a woman who means a great deal to you who has no idea, she turns up at a restaurant, she's gonna be on a mostly blind date. That means I got the greenlight from you. So how deep did you and your boys dive?"

"She deserves no drama," Lee said instead of answering direct.

"Man, if this works out, my guess is it's all in the family. So you and your boys have this about me and I gotta know how much *this* is."

He had to give it to him.

And if the tables were turned, he'd want to know too.

"We know your wife cheated on you with her high school boyfriend at their reunion. You couldn't go. You were at a mandatory cop convention in San Francisco. You found out because you saw an email that led to you lookin' into it and finding more. She contended she got very drunk and wasn't in control of her actions. Guests at the reunion confirm the inebriation is true, but we all know it's no excuse. Still, you went into counseling with her to save your family. Six months into counseling, when you discovered she continued talking to the guy after you found out about the cheat and went into counseling, you decided you couldn't trust her again or save your marriage, which meant your family. By that time, she was all in to save the marriage, if not the family. She made that and the fact she wasn't pleased with your decision plain with four years of divorce court torture."

"Holy shit," Richardson whispered.

"We're thorough," Lee muttered.

"That it?" Richardson asked.

"Army record. Employment records. Your girls have a lot of shit up on Facebook and they need a lesson on privacy settings."

Richardson's mouth got tight.

Lee had a feeling that lesson would occur that night.

"It was invasive and we had good reason. But it ends here," Lee assured. "You get yourself to Barolo Grill, we're out. Now the Rock Chicks, I can't make any promises."

"These 'Rock Chicks,' they're you and your men's women?"

"They're nuts, *and* they're my wife's posse. And Shirleen is one of them."

He began to look less annoyed and more curious.

"It really crazy enough to have books written about it?" he asked.

"My wife was kidnapped…three times."

"Fucking hell," Richardson muttered.

"And I lost track of the explosions."

His eyes got big before he burst out laughing.

Lee didn't find anything funny.

"Let's avoid any of that with you and Shirleen," he ordered on a suggestion.

Richardson was still smiling when he replied, "I'm in on that."

"Tuesday," Lee stated.

Richardson nodded. "Tuesday."

Lee nodded back and turned to his truck.

"Nightingale," Richardson called.

Lee turned back.

"As fucked as it is considering you know more about why my marriage ended than my mother, still, think I owe you," Richardson remarked.

Lee hoped so.

"We'll see."

"Yeah," Richardson replied. "We will."

FOUR

I KNOW IT GOOD

Shirleen

Tuesday night...

"I'm here to meet my girls. Reservation under India Nightingale," I said to the hostess only to watch her eyes get big right before her face closed down.

Damn.

What had those women gotten up to?

I looked to my watch.

I was only seven minutes late.

Then again, they were the Rock Chicks. Seven minutes of them being there—one of them, or all of them—it was a wonder the restaurant wasn't on fire.

"Right this way," the hostess said, giving me a small, courteous smile and moving into the restaurant.

I followed her, tucking my gunmetal Rebecca Minkoff envelope clutch under my arm, staring at my shoes and thinking it was good the girls organized a night out. That meant I got to wear my Alexander Wang beaded slingbacks. I'd been obsessed with wearing them since I met Moses (notthinkingaboutMoses, notthinkingaboutMoses, alwaystotallythinkingaboutMoses).

Not to mention carry that kickass clutch.

I'd turned my attention to the hostess's shoes as she guided the way to the table, thinking they were a little bit of all right and I'd ask her where she got them when she turned and murmured, "Careful of the carpet."

"Thanks," I replied, lifting my eyes to her face.

She gave me another polite smile before again turning forward.

I looked beyond her, wondering why things seemed calm and sedate, considering the Rock Chicks were in the house.

No one was shouting, crying, whooping, laughing so loud the windows shook, and I heard no loud conversations about sex.

I supposed this *was* Barolo Grill.

We were a crazy bunch of bitches but we could get our game faces on when getting thrown out might mean you wouldn't get to eat your *risotto alla milanese* (yes, I had pre-checked the menu, and yes, I totally knew every course I was ordering—all four of them).

I just hadn't decided what cocktail I was going to start with.

What I had decided was that when I had the ambience of Barolo Grill around me, I'd go where the spirit moved me.

This was my thought when the spirit moved me to jack my ass around and take off running the other way.

And this was because the hostess was not leading me to the Rock Chicks.

She was leading me to a table where Moses Richardson was rising from his chair, eyes locked on me. He was wearing a black shirt, a superbly cut dark-gray blazer, crisp jeans, and he looked good enough to eat.

Way better than the four-course meal I'd picked out.

All right.

What...

In *the fuck*...

Was going on?

I didn't run. I couldn't run. And not because I was in a fancy restaurant and wearing high heels (and I was thanking God I'd chosen the black body-con, midi dress with the bateau neck and art deco pattern that, yes, even I could say *I rocked*).

Because Moses Richardson was watching me walk his way, looking fine, looking alert (which was also fine) and looking like he might chase me if I ran.

"Your dinner partner for this evening," the hostess murmured when we stopped at his table. "Enjoy," she finished, then she wasted no further time and took off.

She didn't even motion to one of the chairs or hand me the menu that was sitting on one of the two plates.

I stared at Moses.

He watched me.

I kept staring at Moses thinking Indy had phoned me her damned self to set this up.

But I'd talked with Daisy, Jules and Ava about that night and what we were all wearing.

I'd been played.

By the Rock Chicks *and* the Hot Bunch.

Those boys had *such* big mouths.

I should have known this was not a Rock Chick night. Barolo Grill was Indy and Lee's place (though I didn't know how, I'd made fifteen reservations for them here, and for one reason or another in the life of an RCHB, one of them was always cancelling).

"You're not running away," Moses observed.

"I'm too busy plotting multiple murders."

He smiled.

Lordy.

He moved to pull a chair out.

"Are you going to sit?" he asked.

"I haven't decided yet," I answered.

He settled in while standing there. "I've got all night."

And he looked like he did. He looked like he didn't give a shit we were both standing, staring at each other at a table at the swanky-ass Barolo Grill.

"If I ran, would you chase me?" I asked curiously.

"Yes," he answered.

Hmm.

"Please sit down, Shirleen," he said in that honey voice.

It was the "please" that got me.

I shifted his way, turned, aimed my ass at the chair and sat.

He helped me bring my chair under the table.

Right.

Did I just do that?

Why did I just do that?

I should not have done that.

I set my clutch to the table only because it was in my hand and I was going to push up on it to get out of my chair.

"I should—" I began.

Honey poured into my ear because his lips were *right there*.

Which meant it felt like it poured down my neck.

And south.

"Just relax. It's a man and a woman having dinner. Enjoying each other's company. In this moment, what goes from here doesn't matter. Just be in the now...with me."

I drew in a deep breath.

A man and a woman having dinner.

A juvenile corrections officer and an ex-drug dealer having dinner.

I couldn't do it.

My whole body tensed to bolt.

The honey came back.

"In the now, Shirleen."

I turned my head and looked into his eyes.

"You're not in the now," he told me when his gaze caught mine. "You're in the past. Or you're in the future. The now is just this table. Food. Wine. Conversation. And then it's done."

"What are we gonna talk about?" I asked.

"Whatever you want." He kept hold on my gaze. "And nothing that you don't want."

"You're being very accommodating," I noted.

"I want to have dinner with you."

He wanted to have dinner with me.

This beautiful man wanted to have dinner *with me*.

Could I be in the now?

Not in the past?

(I didn't care about the future.)

I stared into those eyes.

Then I looked away and left my clutch on the table as I grabbed my napkin to put it in my lap.

Moses walked around the table and sat across from me.

I tried to deep breathe without appearing to breathe deep.

The waiter arrived.

Thank the Lord.

"Would we like to start with a cocktail?" he asked.

"Bellini, please," I ordered, leaving off the "and keep them coming."

"Peroni," Moses ordered.

The waiter nodded. "I'll leave you with your menus and be right back."

Moses didn't watch him walk away.

He looked at me.

"So which one do I kill first?" I asked.

"Pardon?" he asked back.

I lifted a hand and whirled it in the air, indicating the table. "Who was the ringleader that arranged this? Indy? Daisy?"

"Lee."

My hand dropped to my lap. "Say what?"

"Lee. He made the approach and he made the reservation. He also made it clear he would not get his wife or your friends involved if he didn't have to. But apparently he had to."

I could not believe this.

"Liam 'Badass isn't my middle name, it's my way of life' Nightingale is playing matchmaker?"

Moses grinned at me and my heart died a little.

"Yep," he answered.

I was shocked.

Okay, freaked.

And that was the entirety of my dinner conversation.

Which made me even more freaked.

I stared at my clutch on the table.

It was a hot clutch.

I still didn't think I could stare at it for an hour over dinner with a hot guy.

"You might want to read your menu," Moses suggested. "It'll give you something to do while you try to think of something to say."

My gaze snapped to him. "So you got practice with this, do you?"

He shot me another smile. "Been divorced for eleven years, Shirleen, and in that time did not enter the priesthood."

I wished he wouldn't smile. It was annoying because it wasn't annoying.

It was amazing.

I took up my menu even though I already knew what I was going to order.

"Get what you want," he stated like it was a command. "And if you even consider suggesting we go dutch, rethink. There'll be consequences you try to pull something like that."

I looked to him again. "Do you threaten all your dates at the beginning of the date?"

"Only ones I think might be difficult, that being only you."

I made a noise that sounded like a humph and then wished I hadn't humphed.

I decided to check out my menu again.

I was pretending to consider my options when Moses asked, "What are the boys doing tonight?"

I didn't repeat my mistake of looking at him again.

I answered my menu.

"Roam, probably his latest girlfriend. Sniff, probably a two-fer, one already down, one on the go, and if he's got time, he'll find a third one and get that action in before he has to be home for curfew."

"Seriously?"

At his tone, I looked to him.

Yep.

His face matched his tone.

I decided I should try to make him think I was at least a decent foster carer.

"My friend Hank keeps them in condoms," I shared.

His brows went high. "And you're okay with this?"

"Hell no," I replied. "I don't even want to be *talking* about this. Though I am because I can't quit *thinking* about it since I ride the razor's edge of one of them getting a girl in trouble. Or getting a girl in so deep she becomes a stalker, something not only they'll have to deal with, but I'll have to deal with her crazy ass too. Or getting a girl whose parents aren't all that big on young love, so their father comes to my house with a shotgun."

"These are all valid concerns," he decreed.

"No shit?" I said by way of agreement. "And they're the only ones I'll let myself think about. What really scares the snot outta me is that the first part of their lives hasn't been sunshine and rainbows. I want the next part to be what they want it to be. I don't want them forced into a situation they have to cope with. I want them free and clear to make the decisions about who they're gonna be and the kind of lives they want to lead."

That bakery-oven goodness wafted over me across the table.

Lord.

I'd always wanted to live somewhere where there was no snow.

That just proved I could bask in warmth the rest of my days. Especially that kind.

"Do you know for a fact they're having sex?" Moses asked.

I tried a trick that Ally often tried.

"La la la," I chanted, looking back down to my menu. "I'm sorry I started it but now this conversation isn't happening."

"Shirleen," he called, and I was forced out of politeness (okay, the proximity of his hotness) to look at him again. "You need to tell them to abstain."

I stared at him.

Then I threw back my head and burst out laughing.

When I was done laughing, I saw he didn't share in the joke.

Still, he said, "First, you're gorgeous when you laugh."

I was?

"Second," he went on, "I neglected to tell you I really like that dress."

Every inch of skin under said dress got hot.

"And last," he continued, "I wasn't being funny."

"When did you lose your virginity?" I asked.

That shut him up.

"Mm-hmm," I murmured, turning my attention back to the menu I had no intention of reading since I'd memorized it that afternoon when I should (probably) have been sending invoices.

"I wasn't a father with two teenage daughters back then."

Oh my God.

My eyes again went to his. "I should tell them that."

"Sorry?"

"I should tell them to catapult themselves into the future thirty years and give themselves teenage daughters," I explained and nearly clapped my hands, but considering the Ritz factor around me, decided against it. "Hot damn, that's perfect. They might listen to that."

They might not.

But they also might.

Well, Sniff probably wouldn't.

But Roam might.

(Maybe.)

"Glad I could give you a new strategy," Moses said.

"I'm glad you could too, though I don't hold high hopes."

He shot me another grin. "I wouldn't be able to see past my hormones at eighteen either."

I thought back to when I was eighteen.

I was dating Leon when I was eighteen.

I quit thinking about when I was eighteen.

"Why don't you just tell them that part about wanting them to be in the position to make the decisions about what's next in their lives?" he asked.

I gave up on the menu and set it aside before I answered, "Because I don't like to remind them that they were forced into the position to do something about the early part of their lives, that bein' becoming runaways."

"Are their parents in the picture at all?"

"No. They. Are. *Not*."

At my words, more I suspected at how I spoke them, fire lit in his eyes. The same fire that I felt burning inside me anytime I thought of Roam's and Sniff's parents.

It took time for the stories to come out. They both told Jules before they told me.

But then they told me.

And that was that.

I never made them speak of it again.

And that was when I retired my switchblade.

Too much of a temptation.

For certain.

But it was not good that with four words, Moses understood and shared that emotion with me for two boys he didn't know. It was not good he was that kind of man. It was not good that kind of man was sitting across the table, having dinner with me.

It was not good because it was beautiful and I knew I wanted more, more of that, more of coming to know how much better he could get.

"That bad?" Moses asked quietly, taking me out of my thoughts.

"Worse," I said sharply.

At this point, fortunately, the cocktails arrived. The waiter then ran down the specials, through which I chanted "la la la" again (but only in my head) because I didn't want him to take me off target.

We ordered and I was pleased Moses ordered all different food from me.

What could I say? It was a thing. If he ordered the same as me, I'd have to change mine and I'd been looking forward to my choices since I made them at two o'clock that afternoon.

And no, this was not so I could taste all he got (even though it was, or it would be with anyone else), just that I couldn't even begin to think of eating off Moses Richardson's plate. The room would get too hot for me to breathe.

"So what are the boys *really* doing tonight?" Moses asked when the waiter moved away.

I was sipping my Bellini.

Yes, I needed those to keep coming, and not just so I could get through this date.

It was *delicious*.

I put it down and answered, "They're manning the control room at the office tonight while doing their homework."

"The control room?"

"Where the men do surveillance at Nightingale Investigations. They're kind of interns."

"That seems...unusual for high school boys," he stated carefully.

"They need good male role models. And there they have a lot of them."

"I see," he murmured. "Is that going to be what's next in their lives?"

I shrugged. "I hope so."

Another grin from Moses. "You like herding badasses."

And so he obviously had his answer about what I'd shared during the grocery store incident.

He was also right. I liked herding badasses.

What I liked more was the fact that, if Lee took them on permanent-like, I'd see my boys every day. Even when they moved out, I'd see them at work and thus could keep tabs on them (and ride their asses) for the foreseeable future.

"Yes," I replied.

The look on Moses's face said he'd read my thoughts but he was smart enough not to comment on them.

I grabbed my Bellini again and took a sip.

When I put it down, I realized I didn't have anything else to say.

I mean, I did.

I could ask about his daughters. I could ask about his job. I could ask if he'd seen *Tarzan* or *300* or *The Accountant* and assess his taste. I could ask why his wife was stupid enough to lose him, or learn he wasn't as perfect as he seemed, had done something stupid and he'd lost her.

But I didn't want to know any of that. I didn't want to know if he was even more fabulous. I didn't want to know if he could be less fabulous, but it would confirm he was human.

I didn't want anything that might make this hurt more when it was over.

"You do know, I know who you are."

My attention went from my Bellini to his face, and I felt my lips had parted.

"I know you're Shirleen Jackson," he carried on. "I know who your husband was. I know what you and your nephew did before you stopped doing it."

I continued to stare at him with my mouth open, but now my throat was burning and there was so much pressure in my head, I thought it would explode.

I should have run.

But since I didn't, I should do it now.

I just couldn't move.

He leaned into the table, staring right back at me.

"So let's get this out there and get past it right now," he kept going. "I don't care, Shirleen. That was who you were. I'm sitting across the table with the woman you are now."

"You...you know that I—?"

Moses cut me off. "I know about the drugs. I know about the poker games. I know about the bar you no longer own and what ran through there. And I know that's all done."

I pressed my lips together.

"We clear on that?" he asked.

I swept up my drink again, looking away.

I took a sip.

It didn't help the burn in my throat.

I should have ordered three all up front.

"Shirleen—"

I turned back to him and put my drink down. "You know that doesn't change the fact that this is it, and then we're never seeing each other again."

His brows drew together. "Why not?"

"Because that will always be there."

"It isn't here now."

I blinked at him.

"If it's not here now, why would it ever be here?" he asked.

Was he crazy?

"I..." I shook my head. "It never goes away," I explained.

He nodded once and sat back. "So you got out of that shit so you could continue to let it control your life and inform who you are?"

That sounded stupid.

"Of course not."

"So why are you letting it control your life and inform who you are?" he pushed.

"It isn't that easy," I told him.

"It wouldn't be that easy if you got out of the game you were in to run guns or peddle flesh or hire yourself out as a hitman, or sorry, hitwoman. Or if you wallowed in the mistakes you made and spent your life drinking yourself to death while watching shows about serial killers on TV. You didn't do any of that. You did it the hard way. You scraped all the shit off and got yourself a decent job with decent people and became a foster mother."

I snatched up my drink at that last.

This was because I was a foster carer.

Unofficially.

Officially, I was an ex-drug dealer, current office manager who'd had two runaways placed with her by means that were a little bit shady (okay, totally shady as in, probably illegal and definitively not through any valid channels).

Luckily, Roam and Sniff both were eighteen now so they were of age and could be anywhere they wanted to be...

And he was a JCO. No, he was Director of Juvenile Probation.

He probably lived and breathed valid channels.

"Shirleen," he called.

I looked at him while gulping back a glug of Bellini.

"I know it wasn't above board, how you got those boys. I don't care about that either," he declared.

I took the glass from my mouth but didn't set it back on the table.

There was less than half left, but I needed it close.

"What *do* you care about?" I asked.

And I'd find that I shouldn't have.

Alternately, it could turn out it was the best thing I'd done in my life.

Because he answered.

Thoroughly.

"I care that my daughters get through high school without some hormonal boy making me a grandfather ten years before I'm ready for that shit, and also ruining my record of living fifty-one years of life without murdering a teenager. I care about them making decisions that will lead to happiness, not wealth or status or designer clothes, not drugs or booze or men who treat them like garbage."

These were good things to care about, I thought.

Real good.

Moses didn't give me the chance to make comment.

He kept going.

"I care about the turkey being cooked just right on Thanksgiving. Juicy goodness for the meal and days of leftover turkey sandwiches. I care about staying healthy for the day at least ten years away when my grandchildren come and I can put them on my shoulders and keep up with them when we're horsing around. I care that my toilets don't run and my faucets don't leak and my yard looks good because I like to come home to a house that's well maintained with a yard that looks good. But also I think everyone should be the kind of neighbor that cares for their home, and cares enough for their neighbors no one has to look at a shitty-ass yard when they come home."

This was all good too.

Especially the turkey and home maintenance parts.

Who was I kidding?

Especially the taking care of himself part.

(But the turkey was a good one.)

Moses didn't stop.

"I care about the Broncos and hope they win another Super Bowl, or twenty of them before I die. I care about global warming because I'm scared as shit about what my daughters and their children are going to face if we don't sort our asses out. I care about the kids at my center and hope like fuck every one of them finds the righteous path, even if I have enough experience to know that not many of them will because their parents are for shit."

He leaned in again and not that he'd taken his eyes from mine as he was giving this speech, but the way he started looking at me nailed me right to the spot.

"And this minute, I care about talking a beautiful woman, in a gorgeous dress with the most badass head of hair I've seen in my life and the most amazing eyes I've ever looked into who has a golden soul she hasn't become acquainted with yet, into letting shit go so she not only enjoys this dinner with me, she lets me take her to a movie on Thursday."

"You already want a second date?" I whispered.

"I already want a lot more from you, Shirleen Jackson, but I'm gonna remain focused on the short run in hopes I can stretch it long so maybe one day you can taste my Thanksgiving turkey. I make the best turkey, baby. So good, you'll want Thanksgiving to come every day."

"You brine it?" I was still whispering.

"Absolutely."

"Roast it with stuffing?"

He nodded his head. "Mm-hmm."

"I like the way you look at me."

Unh-hunh, still whispering.

"I like the way you look sitting across from me," he replied.

"I never want to see your face looking at me any other way than how you're looking at me right now."

The bakery-oven goodness shot across the table as a blast of heat while understanding seeped into his eyes.

"You ever gonna deal drugs again?" he asked gently.

"That wouldn't be a very good example to Roam and Sniff and the foster grandbabies I hope they give me in no less than ten years."

"I'm thinkin' 'foster' doesn't really factor anymore, baby."

I shut up.

God, wouldn't that be *heaven*?

"You gonna go to a movie with me on Thursday?" he pressed.

"I'm not sure I'll be able to make it through the appetizer," I admitted.

He looked confused. "I thought we were getting somewhere."

"You terrify me, Moses Richardson."

That wasn't a blurt.

I said that cognizant of each word that came out of my mouth.

He did not take it as intended.

He looked pleased with himself.

Seriously pleased.

It was his best look yet.

Oowee.

"I know how to settle you down," he assured.

Lordy.

"That's what terrifies me," I pointed out.

He grinned, and it was not like any of the other ones he'd given me.

My toes curled in my Alexander Wang's.

"You're very sure of yourself," I noted.

The promise went out of his face and something else set in it before he refuted me.

"No I'm not. The only thing I'm sure of is that I want to get to know you better, Shirleen, in a variety of ways. I don't know how this is gonna go. I don't know where this is gonna go. I don't know how deep you're gonna let me in. I just know I want to give us a shot, which means I want you with me in doing that. That's all I know. But I know it good."

I looked deep into his eyes.

It isn't here now.

"You got pictures of your girls?" I asked.

That didn't get me a blast of bakery-oven goodness.

A cool breeze drifted across the table emanating from the relief in his eyes, and I watched the tension leaving his shoulders as he sat back, regarding me.

"Only about seven thousand two hundred of them," he answered.

"Then whip out your phone, my man," I invited.

The warmth came back in his smile as he reached inside his blazer to pull out his phone.

Moses Richardson did not have seven thousand two hundred pictures of his daughters.

He had nine thousand two hundred of them.

They were beautiful.

And as he spoke of them, I realized that beauty ran deep.

So it was clear they got a lot from their dad.

I HAD no earthly clue how I was sitting next to Moses Richardson in his truck.

Yes, I did.

I'd planned to have a few drinks at dinner with the girls, and the boys had need of my Navigator, so I'd Ubered it there.

And after dinner, when he'd found out I did, he would hear nothing but me allowing him to plant my ass right where it was so he could drive me home.

We were going to a movie on Thursday.

He loved 300 and thought *The Accountant* was the shit.

"That belt scene, baby," he'd drawled. "Bad...*ass*."

Though he hadn't seen *Tarzan* and shared he had no intention to, but asked, "You like yourself some white boys?"

"He's six foot four," was my reply, and if Moses had a vagina (which thankfully he did not), he would understand this was all I had to say.

Moses had no reply to my reply.

Clearly I had to say more.

"And his portrayal of Eric Northman adheres to my philosophy on how to be a vampire."

A surprised chuckle bubbled from him as he asked, "You've got a philosophy on how to be a vampire?"

"Who doesn't?" I asked back.

Moses again had no reply, but this time he did it looking like he was trying real hard not to bust a gut laughing.

"It's simple," I stated.

"Share," he urged.

I did.

"Own it. You're gonna live forever and gotta do that by drinkin' blood and raisin' hell, why not? Live it up. Go for the gusto. Bust it out. And make no apologies."

"Maybe there's somethin' for you to learn from this fictional vampire guy," he'd said quietly.

That was when I had no reply.

Until I did.

"There you go, making it all deep."

"I don't know what's deeper than finding out what kind of vampire a woman would wanna be."

And that was when I burst out laughing.

That had been it.

After a rocky start, it was good conversation with delicious food and cocktails that led into fantastic wine, and now my ass was beside his in his truck where he was driving me home.

How did this happen?

One second, I was "puttin' on the Ritz" to hit the town with my girls.

The next, I was sitting beside a hot guy in his truck after having a good date.

No, a great date.

No, a fabulous date.

Damn.

"We'll hold hands at the movie theater, but tonight, baby, I'll just walk you to the door. So you can settle down. It's been beautiful and I don't want you to get all nervous now. That would fuck it up."

I turned my head to look at him.

The last thing Leon Jackson did before he left our home and then got whacked was backhand me into a wall.

And I knew without asking, the man sitting beside me had never raised a hand to a woman.

Hell, he might never have raised his hand to a man, unless he was sparring with him at his boxing gym (I did not know if Moses belonged to a boxing gym, but it was a good thought).

He glanced at me, his beautiful lips quirked, before looking back at the road.

"You good?" he asked.

What did I say?

My dead husband regularly beat the shit out of me? And the last years of our marriage, sex was more like habitual rape since I never wanted it but he took it anyway, and by then I'd learned not to fight it? And since the man got dead, I got myself a little somethin'-somethin' here and there but it never lasted and it never meant anything? Now I'm sitting next to Moses and I worked with good men. And through them and my friends, I witnessed every day how a functional, loving relationship survived.

But I had no clue what I was doing and how I got my ass here beside him.

"Shirleen?" he prompted.

I turned forward.

"Okay, baby," he said gently, "we'll let whatever you got goin' in that head of yours slide."

Thank the Lord.

"For now," he finished.

Shit.

He drove.

I sat beside him listening to the soothing strains of vintage R&B punctuated with his GPS guiding him to my driveway since he made me give him my address to program it in (okay, he didn't "make me," as such—he asked and I gave him my address), as well as my phone number.

He let the silence settle, and I had a feeling it was all right with him. Moses struck me as a man who could be comfortable in silence.

I was not.

He pulled into my drive, put the truck in park, turned it off and then twisted to me.

"Boys home?" he asked.

I shook my head. "I told them to text me when they got home.

They've learned to do that without fail. And they haven't done that, so no."

"I'm walking you to your door."

Moses bringing up my boys made me think of them and the fact they wouldn't be home any time soon since it wasn't yet eleven and that was their curfew when they were working at NI.

But maybe Jack at the office who usually manned the control room for the night shift was feeling some alone time and let them go early.

This was my last thought before Moses opened my door.

The man opened a woman's car door.

Oh sweet Lord.

He offered me his hand.

I took it and the warmth and strength of his long fingers wrapping around mine made me freeze solid as I stared at our hands. His unrelentingly masculine, mine had long fingers, rounded knuckles with the skin darker there, my nails long and now coated in a silvery metallic with a hint of soft purple.

And staring at them, it hit me there was nothing more beautiful than two clasped hands.

"Shirleen?"

I tore my eyes from our hands and forced myself to shift my body to get out of his truck.

He held me gripped tight as I negotiated my dismount.

And he kept hold on me as he guided me out of the door, closed it, and walked me up to my front door.

He stopped us there and I stared at it so I wouldn't turn my head and stare at him.

Or burst out crying.

Because there I was, Shirleen Jackson, fifty-three, with my history, being walked to her front door after the best date I'd had in my life.

"Uh, baby."

Forced to do so due to manners, when Moses called, I turned my head.

Yep.

Best date of my life.

"You got the key?" he asked.

It was then, I didn't know what came over me.

Well, I knew what came over me. I just didn't know how I let it come over me.

You see, I tugged my hand free from his.

Then I put my hands to either side of his head and pulled it down to mine.

And I kissed him.

His beard was bristly.

But his lips were soft.

I slid my tongue between them.

Lord God, he tasted of *panna cotta* and man.

Nothing more beautiful had ever touched my tongue.

Overwhelmed by it, I shoved him back until he hit the side wall to the alcove that shadowed my front door, protecting it from the elements.

And I kissed the ever-lovin' hell out of Moses Richardson.

Then suddenly I wasn't kissing the ever-lovin' hell out of him.

Even though I was pressed up to his big, solid body having shoved him into a wall, his arms were tight around me, his head had slanted, and he was kissing the ever-lovin' hell out of *me*.

Oowee *God*!

Shirleen was dizzy!

Suddenly (and regrettably) I became conscious of the fact that I was a woman raising two boys and I had neighbors.

So I tore myself out of his arms, took a step back, and smoothed my dress down my hips.

"Uh…" I mumbled.

I found my jaw cupped by a big warm hand and a handsome face right in mine.

"How we feelin' about watchin' that movie on my couch?" he asked, the honey gone, all that was there was smooth gravel.

Lord.

"Um, I'm thinkin', uh..."

I couldn't finish because what I was thinking about was lying-down couch action and if one of the boys would miss it if I took a condom or two.

No, no, no. A woman did not steal condoms from her boys.

That was what drugstores were for.

And anyway, wasn't that Moses's territory?

I didn't know. It had been too long.

And I wasn't asking a Rock Chick as I'd decided I wasn't speaking to them (any of them) for at least a week.

"We'll pick a movie for both and decide Thursday," he stated.

"Sounds like a plan," I forced out.

"That was a nice kiss," he murmured.

"Um, yeah," I murmured back.

"*Real* nice."

"Uh..."

His eyes started twinkling. "Never been body slammed into fake adobe before."

My eyes narrowed.

His eyes roamed over my face and hair and the look in them changed.

"Fuck, could you get more perfect?" he whispered.

I went solid.

His gaze locked onto mine. "Don't go back there."

"Moses."

"In the now."

"I'm not—"

"In the now, right now, after that kiss, you bein' so cute, you... are...*perfect*."

Hell and damn.

I wanted to cry again.

He bent in, brushed his lips across the apple of my cheek and pulled away, dropping his hand from my jaw, and the loss of it felt like the loss of a limb.

I drew in a steadying breath.

He bent and nabbed the Minkoff clutch I hadn't noticed I dropped.

"Please tell me there's a key in there," he joked, offering my bag to me.

I took it, opened it and slid the key out.

I held it up and showed it to him.

He took it from me and turned to the door.

Then Moses Richardson, like a gentleman, let me into my own house.

Of course, I had to push in to reach and punch in the code for the alarm that was beeping.

But still, the move was smooth.

And it was sweet.

Like honey.

Like Moses.

Standing just inside my door, I turned to him.

He moved close and rested a hand on my waist.

"Please don't kiss me again," I begged in a whisper.

"No way," he replied. "I'd rather not meet your boys when I got you naked on the tile of your foyer."

I huffed out a breath that I wanted to be a huff of irritation, but it was more a huff of relief because I didn't want that either.

Though I did.

Just not the meeting my boys while it was happening part.

He knew what it was and smiled at me.

Then he bent in and I sucked in breath while he touched his lips to the skin right in front of my ear.

He pulled away.

"Great night, Shirleen. Perfect."

"Mm-hmm," was the only thing I trusted to move between my lips.

"Thursday, baby."

I nodded.

His fingers at my waist gave me a squeeze.

After that, he turned and I watched him walk away.

He wasn't as fabulous from the behind as from the front.

But it was a close call.

He got in his truck and gave me a finger flick before he pulled out.

I was closing the door as he was driving away.

Once I got the door closed, I locked it.

Then I put my forehead to it.

I closed my eyes.

After that kiss, you bein' so cute, you...are...perfect.

I opened my eyes.

And like I was addled...

I smiled—huge—at my own damned door.

FIVE

BLESSINGS

Shirleen

The next morning, I walked into the offices.

I didn't miss a step as I marched to my desk, regardless of the fact that Luke Stark had his thigh leaned against the extension where my computer was, Vance Crowe had his ass up on the corner, Kai "Mace" Mason was leaning against the opposite end, Hector Chavez was lounged on the couch across from it, boots on the coffee table...

And Lee Nightingale was sitting in my damned desk chair, leaned back, elbows to the chair arms, his hands linked on his abs.

"Well?" Luke asked.

"Sss!" I hissed, moving directly to my occupied chair.

"Give it up, Shirleen," Vance ordered.

I lifted my hand, slapped my fingers against my thumb at him and snapped, "Zzzp!"

I stopped. Dumped my Prada on the desk. And put my hands to my hips to glare down at Lee.

He didn't move.

Though his mouth did.

"Indy called you seven times last night."

"Ava called five," Luke put in.

"Jules called three," Vance added.

"Sadie called Indy, Ava, Daisy and Jules repeatedly," Hector stated from the couch.

"Stella and me were out to dinner with Roxie and Hank, and those two were manning their texts like they were planning the Normandy invasion through them," Mace shared.

I swung an arm out to indicate all five men.

"I'm not talkin' to all you all," I declared.

"Indy only let up when Roam and Sniff got home and checked in on you after I told them to do that," Lee announced.

My eyes got huge and I forgot I wasn't talking to him.

"You told my boys to check in on me?"

"They said you were in bed, reading," Lee replied. "And I took that as I didn't have to go out and murder someone for bein' a dick to my girl."

So that was why they knocked on the door and stuck their heads in.

Both of them.

Usually it was just a shouted, "We're home, Shirleen!"

"What excuse did you use to tell them they had to check in on me?" I asked.

"As far as they knew, you were out with the Rock Chicks. They always check in on you after you're out with the Rock Chicks. They didn't think anything of it since my wife is a Rock Chick, you were supposed to be out with her, and who knows what you all get up to."

"What, with stun gunning and car chases not out of the ordinary," Luke filled in.

This made sense.

And this was true. Whenever I was in after being out with the Rock Chicks, one or the other of my boys checked in physically.

Just not both of them.

"You're in my chair," I pointed out to Lee.

"Technically, it's my chair," he returned.

This was true too.

Fine.

He wanted to play it that way?

I picked up my bag, mumbling, "I've been meaning to take some time off."

"Shirleen, you can have your chair back when you tell us how it went last night," Lee stalled me.

"Who says I want my chair back?" I asked. "Maybe I want to call Daisy and have some brunch before we go shopping."

"Daisy's at work at Ally's office, and anyway, I know you're not talkin' to her since she called you last night, ten times, and you didn't answer her either," Lee retorted.

"The girls bought themselves Shirleen's Patented Silent Treatment for a whole week for their shenanigans," I shot back.

Suddenly, Lee's expression shifted.

And I'd become accustomed to a lot from these men. Their hotness. Their sweetness with their women. Their occasional scariness when they got pissed or on edge.

Even so, I took a mini step back at the look that hit his face.

And the tone of his voice I'd never heard in my life and I'd known Lee since he was a teenager.

"You didn't have a good time?"

"We're going to a movie tomorrow night."

Lee relaxed.

"So you had a good time," Mace growled.

I drew in a big breath and let it out on a sigh.

"Yeah," I told Mace. "He's nice. He's handsome. He didn't blink at me ordering a four-course meal at an expensive restaurant and he was right there with me. So we're gonna take in a movie tomorrow." I then glared at Mace. "Happy?"

Broody Mace left the building and he smiled at me. "Yeah."

I turned back to Lee. "Now will you get outta my chair? I got invoices to send."

Or not.

I was feeling the need to have a new outfit for movie night. An outfit I could order online and pick up at Nordstrom on the way home.

"So it's all good," Lee noted, straightening his long body out of my chair.

"The *date* was all good," I corrected. "You men and your women interfering with my life and setting me up like that was *all bad*."

"Can't be bad if you had a good time," Vance pointed out.

I positioned myself in front of the chair Lee had vacated and skewered him with my eyes.

"And what if it had been a disaster?" I asked.

"We would have killed him," Vance answered casually.

This might have been sweet, or funny, if it wasn't possibly true.

"You're officially not allowed to kill or maim or otherwise torture Moses Richardson even if things don't work out with us," I decreed.

"So you had a *good time*," Hector remarked, having risen from the couch to stand between Mace and Vance in front of my desk.

He was grinning.

I looked among the testosterone brigade. "You're all pretty pleased with yourselves, aren't you?"

"Pretty much," Luke rumbled.

His lips had formed a half-grin.

Okay, they got what they wanted from their interrogation, it was time for me to shop.

So even as I sat my ass down, I had a hand up, shooing them. "Fine. Now git. This conversation is at an end."

As I spoke, my purse rang.

I reached in, took out my cell, saw the number was local but not programmed in.

As much as I wanted to ignore it because in all likelihood it was someone trying to sell me something, I couldn't.

Local could mean a local marketing call.

It could also mean I forgot I scheduled the boys in for their dental cleaning and the dentist office was calling to remind me, which would be good, since if that was the case, I'd forgotten (mental note: put dentist appointments in planner; second mental note: buy dental appointment stickers). Or the school was calling about something. Or Roam's girlfriend's father was calling to schedule an inter-family meeting to discuss the variety of reasons why chicken and waffles were never happening again.

So I took the call.

"You got Shirleen," I said into my phone.

"Mornin', baby," Moses said into my ear.

Heat and goose bumps both fought for control of the surface of my skin.

"Hey," I whispered, my eyes dropping to my desk, but that desk, the office, the men and the world had vanished.

Everything had become Moses.

He was calling me the morning after a date.

No messing about for him making me wait to hear his voice, pretending he didn't want to connect with me, letting me know right away I was on his mind.

"How'd you sleep?" he asked.

"Good," I lied.

I didn't sleep.

I kept reliving that kiss, the sound of his laughter, the sight of his smiles, his words about me being perfect over and over again.

It was the best sleepless night in history.

"Good," he replied. "So, might be too early for a home date, but I got a slow-cook brisket recipe that'll knock your socks off. I introduce you to that, you introduce me to *Tarzan*. Work for you?"

I loved brisket.

"Alternately, the Mayan has a retrospective screening of *Set It Off*. We can hit The Hornet after," he went on.

Oowee!

Latifah, Jada, Vivica and Kimberly?

Oh no.

How was I going to decide between brisket or Latifah?

"Too much goodness, my man," I told him. "I can't pick."

"You know I'm gonna choose you bein' on my couch, even if I have to watch a white boy swing from a tree."

I burst out laughing, this making me look up, this reminding me I had an audience who had not, I was not surprised to note, *shooed*.

Damn.

I had five sets of hot-guy eyes on me in varying degrees of amusement and warmth.

But it was Lee who approached me.

And then it was Lee who bent down and kissed my forehead.

Yes.

You read that right.

Lee Nightingale bent down and kissed me, Shirleen Jackson's forehead.

Hell and damnation.

And it was Lee who whispered, "You're welcome."

When he pulled away, I gave him a death glare.

But honestly?

My heart wasn't in it.

He knew this and thus gave me Liam Nightingale's Patented Get-In-Your-Panties Smile.

He had no intention of getting in anyone but Indy's panties, and I had no desire for that.

Still.

It was just the way it came out.

I fought fanning myself and continued to push out the glare.

He wandered away.

His men followed him.

Moses called in my ear, "Shirleen? I lose you?"

"The men were hanging around my desk, annoying me. I had to

give them my death glare to get them to move out, and when I have to pull out the death glare, I need to concentrate," I explained.

He chuckled.

Hearing it, the world suddenly felt right for the first time since Leon Jackson looked across the high school cafeteria at me.

I was in trouble.

Or I was in heaven.

Time would tell which one.

Moses brought me back on target. "*Tarzan* and brisket or Latifah and popcorn followed by bar food?"

Tarzan included his couch, which was a plus and a terrifying minus.

Queen Latifah included a dark movie theater, which would mean no chat, and a possibly loud bar, but definitely other people around, which would mean no meaningful chat.

And I wanted to get to know Moses Richardson.

And maybe, just maybe, I should get what I wanted for a change.

"Brisket," I forced out.

"That was my choice, sweetheart."

Hmm.

"I gotta get back to my kids, but first, tell me how the men are annoying you," he ordered. "Do I have to have a talk with Nightingale?"

I wondered briefly how that would go, and even briefly it was strong enough for me almost to say yes just to find out.

"Maybe we can save you gettin' in his face for when he does something stupid. Like refusing to wear a vest when the mission calls for one," I suggested.

"Does he do that?"

"He loves his wife, his family, wants to make his own one day, and isn't a moron, so…no."

That got me another chuckle before, "Okay then, I'll let you handle the men and I'll go handle my kids. I'll text you my address. Six too early for you?"

If he lived anywhere in the Denver Metro area, a six o'clock date meant I had time to get home and get changed, refresh makeup and check my 'fro and deal with lift, or shrink, and moisture, depending on where the day took it.

And this was fantastic. I could now focus my Nordstrom shopping and not knock him dead with too much fabulousness (but still bring just enough fabulousness) since we were going to be at his house, not out on the town.

"Six works," I replied.

"Right. Text you and call you tonight."

Call me tonight?

When I didn't say anything, he asked, "You got something on tonight?"

Only continuing to phone block all the Rock Chicks.

And maybe door block them if they descended *en masse* at my house, which could happen.

In fact, they were probably planning that right now.

Or ambushing me at the office.

"No," I answered.

"You good with a call?" he pressed.

"I, uh…"

"Wanna get to know you, Shirleen. We don't gotta talk until James Corden comes on, but phone talk is easier than across-a-table talk. Especially in the beginning."

Boy, he had this date shit down.

"It is?"

"Yeah, baby," he said, sounding like he was smiling. "Prove it to you tonight."

"All right, good," I replied quietly. "I'd like that."

"Good."

"Yeah."

"Okay."

"Mm-hmm."

A pause then, "Sweetheart, I'm sorry but I gotta go."

Damn.

"Okay. Yes. Right. I'll let you go."

Another chuckle then, "Talk to you later, Shirleen."

"You sure will, Moses."

"Later, baby."

"Later, uh…Moses."

That got me another chuckle before he disconnected.

I stared at my phone after I took it from my ear, having the strange urge to hold it and what had just been coming from it to my chest.

Then I jumped so high, I nearly fell out of my chair when I heard, "So I don't gotta kill my best friend for settin' my aunt up with some asshole of a brother?"

I lifted my eyes to see my nephew and ex-partner in crime (literally), Darius Tucker, standing at my desk looking like he was trying to attempt X-ray vision as he scowled down at me.

Boy, the power of Moses Richardson was *fierce*. Darius could be silent as a cat but no one got in that room from either door without me knowing.

Normally.

"Those boys tell you they set me up?" I asked.

"Nope," he answered. "Monty told me. Thought it'd be best if shit went south, I was in the know so if some asshole fucked you over that Lee and the guys set you up with, I only had one reason to murder them, not two."

"It went okay, son," I said quietly.

"Just okay?" he asked irritably.

"No. It went real good. He seems like a decent man. So we're having a movie night tomorrow."

"You ever think Leon was a decent man?"

I pressed my lips together.

When Darius's father was murdered, Leon had homed in for the kill, recruiting my nephew to groom him to be his right-hand man, using Darius's grief that manifested as anger to drag him into a life that was not for him. A world he should have never known.

And by then, I was so cowed by my husband I had not saved my nephew from that nightmare.

We'd become partners after Leon had been killed.

In other words, I hadn't saved my nephew from an ongoing nightmare.

"We got things we should hash out, Darius," I said meaningfully.

"No we don't," he returned, as ever, catching his aunt's meaning.

I lifted my chin. "We should have hashed them out ages ago."

He shook his head. "No need. We were both drowning. Can't save someone when you've got two lungs filled with water."

"Son—"

I shut up when he leaned into a fist on my desk.

"You think you should have saved me. I think I should have saved you. And you know what, Aunt Shirleen?"

"What?" I whispered, staring into cold, dark, dead eyes that I hadn't seen looking like that since the bad old days.

He'd been redeemed.

He'd been reunited with his one true love.

He wasn't living the life.

But he was finding his way there.

With Lee's help. The Hot Bunch. The Rock Chicks.

Malia.

And lastly...

His son.

He told me the what.

I just didn't get it.

"On that, I win."

"Come again?"

"I didn't go home to him. I didn't go home to him bustin' my lip or blacking my eye or whatever he did to you that I still feel sick in my gut thinkin' about when you walked funny and wouldn't look anyone in the eye."

I swallowed.

It was good in the bad old days, and now, in the good new ones, Darius was exceptionally observant.

Though I was seeing it might also have been bad.

"So I shoulda saved you," he declared.

"If you tried, you woulda died."

"And that was a result I should have risked if it meant I might have bested it and got you free."

"Darius—"

"But it didn't happen that way and here we are." He pushed off my desk and swung a hand out. "Can't go back. Just gotta move forward."

"No," I disagreed, realizing right then how wise Moses's advice was. "We gotta be in our nows."

"What?"

Holding my nephew's gaze, I stood.

"We gotta be in our nows, son. I met a decent man and he wants a second date. You got a second chance with Malia and your boy. That's our nows. And they're good. So we gotta be where our feet are. Right here. Right now. Not back then, where there's nothin' good, but it doesn't matter, we can't change a thing. Not in the future, which we don't know what's gonna happen and we got no control over it anyway. The now. Right now. Where it's good."

"I always trusted you."

Lord God, I was going to cry.

"Darius."

"I always loved you."

So going to cry.

"Son."

"And the only reason I stayed in was to protect you."

That shut my mouth.

"And I don't regret it," he finished.

"The only reason I stayed in was to protect you," I shared.

"The vicious cycle," he muttered.

"I regret that. The fact you stayed in for me. The fact I stayed in to protect you instead of getting you out. Hell, I regret all of it," I whispered.

"That's not in the now," he pointed out.

"It isn't, you're right," I replied. "But it's still true."

We stood there, staring at each other.

Two sinners.

He'd been redeemed.

But I was so destroyed by the experience, I needed to be reborn.

"Be happy," Darius whispered.

"I'm trying."

"And I'm glad."

With that, as was his way, Darius ended it without another word, moving to the door to the inner sanctum.

He stopped at it and turned my way in order to give me another word.

"Wished I'd killed him myself, what he did to you."

I shook my head. "Don't matter, son. Bottom line, he's dead and it's good it wasn't at your hand."

"I still wished it was."

I got that.

I felt that.

Sometimes, in my darker hours, I thought the same thing.

So I nodded.

My nephew didn't nod back.

He punched in the code to buzz open the door and he walked through.

I stood there watching as the door closed him from sight.

My worst mistake.

Shit.

It was time to go shopping.

I sat, booted up my computer and virtually went to my happy place.

In other words, I hit Nordstrom.

"Okay, lay it on me. What's on your mind?"

It was that evening and we were having a phone conversation, me and Moses.

The boys were at the NI offices, not pulling a shift but working out with Mace in the down room. They'd be home soon and they'd be hungry, which was why I had the hamburger patties already formed, the deep fat fryer out ready to be plugged in to prep for the crinkle cuts, and the tomatoes sliced, the lettuce leaves cleaned, in hopes they'd get some vegetables by dressing their hamburgers with them.

And I was hiding in my bedroom because Moses had called, and when the boys had caught him checking me out at the grocery store, they hadn't liked that much.

They also both gave the roses dirty looks, but I just pretended I bought them myself.

So now I was worried about them coming home to catch me on the phone with him, putting the one of the roses together with the one of me hiding in my room talking on the phone and getting Moses.

But this was only part of the heavy weighing on my mind.

Heavy it was weird that through the miracle of wireless communication, Moses had caught.

"I'm not sure I want to talk about it," I told Moses.

"This is the beauty of the early dating phone conversation. You can talk to me pretending I'm one of your girls."

He seemed sage about this beginning-to-date shit.

But even I hadn't been out of the game long enough to know that was seriously not right.

"My man, ain't no way I can pretend you're one of my girls."

"I know. But I had to give it a shot because I wanna know what's on your mind."

You had to hand it to the brother, he didn't beat around the bush.

"My nephew Darius and me had a convo this morning, and it just...it..." I couldn't finish because I didn't know what to say.

"It just what, sweetheart?" he pressed gently.

"We never talked about some things we probably should have talked about a long time ago."

"And you talked about those things this morning?"

"As much as Darius would let me," I shared. "He isn't a big get-your-feelings-out-there-and-process kind of brother."

"Just in case you haven't figured this out yet, there aren't many brothers who are that kind of brother," Moses pointed out.

I knew that was the truth.

"Though I got no problem with that shit," he added.

Fantastic.

"I know you aren't cool with it, but did he seem cool with it when you got done talking?" he asked.

"We both got regrets."

"Everyone has regrets."

I heard that.

It was just that some were more extreme.

"We both got guilt."

"Shirleen—"

I cut him off. "I know you're gonna say be in the now, but that's my boy and I fucked him up. He was Roam and Sniff's age when it happened and now I got a second chance, and what if I fuck that up?"

"You and your nephew are both on the righteous path and those two boys you got under your roof, Shirleen, you know if their path was going to be different, they would have gone down it by now and they'd be in a different place. Not manning the control room at Nightingale Investigations or goin' grocery shoppin' with their momma. They'd be dealers, rent boys or dead."

I had nothing to say to that, mostly because it was true.

And it gave me the shivers just to think about it.

Moses, however, still had shit to say.

"You say you fucked one up, but he's still standing and he made it to the other side, and he did that with you. But straight up, you *saved* two so I think your record's pretty fuckin' good, baby. Think on that."

I would.

I'd think on that.

Because I liked the way he saw it and I hadn't seen it that way.

"They don't know about you yet," I blurted.

The smile came through when he replied, "I didn't figure you shared about your ambush date over Cream of Wheat this morning."

He could give it straight, I needed to do that too.

"I'm not sure they're gonna be super hip on you."

"They've had you to themselves for a while, Shirleen. But neither of those two struck me as momma's boys, and they might be protective in the beginning, but if this works, I'll win them over in the end."

"I don't think I'm gonna say anything for, you know…a little while. Just, you know…to see. No reason for any drama if there's, uh… eventually no reason for that drama."

"I'm doing the same thing."

I nodded. "Wise."

"When the time comes, though, the girls are gonna love you."

I was not thinking about this.

This was not in my now.

I had enough scary shit in my now. I didn't need to add to it.

"Mm-hmm," I mumbled.

He chuckled.

"I like your laugh," I whispered.

"I like yours too, sweetheart," he whispered back. "Need to get you to a place where I hear it more often."

"I laugh a lot."

"Not around me."

"That's because you're scary as hell."

"That's the place we gotta get you around to get you to the right place."

I tipped my head to the side. "You got this shit down, how many women have you dated since your divorce?"

"I didn't keep track."

"Is that another way of saying you lost count?"

He chuckled again, but did it as he said, "No."

"This is not an answer to my question, Moses."

"I haven't been celibate, but I'm not a player. Promise that, Shirleen. That answer work for you?"

"I 'spose," I mumbled.

"No offense, just getting it out there, but you haven't hidden you're out of practice."

Fabulous.

He kept going, "So we'll take this at your pace, baby. Just as long as we're moving forward for as long as that works for both of us, I don't care how slow we go."

"You know the scariest part about you, Moses?" I asked.

"Hit me with it, Shirleen."

"You seem too good to be true."

There was a weighty pause before, "I'm human. I'm gonna fuck up. Tick you off. Annoy the hell out of you. I'm not givin' you the good stuff and hidin' the bad to get in there. This, where this is at right now, I'm takin' as indication that we got something good to work with. Normally, the red flags fly right off. That said, there'll come a day when you won't feel that. I just hope that day you still feel this foundation we're building and wanna use it to work whatever it is through."

"I can be…a bit much too," I admitted.

Another smile in his voice. "Yeah, and how's that?"

"I can be…stubborn."

That didn't get me a chuckle. He out and out laughed.

"You find that funny?" I asked.

"Baby, you refused to call me, but wanted to, so your boss set us up on a date. But I got the stubborn thing even before that happened."

Well then.

"I sometimes talk about myself in the third person."

Moses was silent.

"It's my thing," I went on.

"And?" he asked after I shut up.

"Some people find that weird."

"So?"

I grinned. "Shirleen's happy you don't find that weird."

He started laughing again.

My phone sounded in my hand telling me I had another call just as I heard shouted by Sniff, "Shirleen, we're home!"

See?

Told you that's how it went down.

"I'm plugging in the deep fat fryer!" he continued.

And see?

Told you they'd come home hungry.

I took the phone away from my ear, saw it said Daisy calling, ignored it and put the phone back to my ear saying, "Hold on a sec."

Then I took it from my ear again.

"I'll be out in a minute!" I shouted.

"Awesome!" Sniff shouted back.

I put the phone to my ear again. "The boys are home."

"That was my guess."

I smiled again.

Then I frowned.

"Means I should let you go," I said. "They were working out with Mace. I gotta get the burgers goin'."

"Then I'll let you go, baby. And I'll see you tomorrow."

"Okay, Moses."

"Do you want me to fire up the grill?" Roam yelled.

I put my hand over the phone and yelled back. "If you wanna grill, won't stop you! But I was gonna fry!"

"Grill!" Sniff bellowed.

"I'll fire it up!" Roam shouted.

"Great!" I yelled.

I took my hand off the phone and heard Moses chuckling again.

"Sorry, that was rude," I mumbled.

"Yep, ain't nothin' foster about that, sweetheart. Sounds just like a family to me. Now I'm lettin' you go. See you tomorrow at my place. Six."

"Okay, Moses, see you then."

"'Bye, baby."

"'Bye, uh...Moses."

He disconnected mid-chuckle again.

I took my phone from my ear and engaged texts.

I then texted Daisy, *Rock Chick freeze out still in operation. I'll tell you about the date and the movie we're watching tomorrow night LATER.*

That'd get her. Her big-haired head would explode knowing we already had a second date planned before she knew one thing about the first.

I got up from my bed and padded in my dress from the office that day but with my slippers on my feet to the door. I opened it, went through and walked down the hall toward the open-plan kitchen that was in the middle of the great room.

During this walk my phone sounded with a text.

Daisy.

You know it don't work that way, sugar.

An extra freeze out day for every text, I replied.

Those three dots that said she was typing didn't even form.

Daisy Sloane knew when I meant business.

Spread the word to the Chicklets, I ordered.

I sent that off and hit the kitchen to see Sniff shoving Doritos in his face.

"Shouldn't you be eating a banana?" I asked.

"Maybe," he answered.

I put a hand on my hip. "You missed this, but every time I say that, that's my way of saying put the junk down and eat a banana."

He grinned at me, teeth filled with Dorito goo, which he knew worked my *last* nerve.

Then he kept eating Doritos.

I could have no idea if this was universal teenage boy or his last hold on rebelling against authority.

My boys were good boys. Even in the beginning, they did what they were told. That had never been a battle.

Of course, at the time, Sniff was with me first since Roam was in the hospital recovering from a gunshot wound. Then Roam was home, with me all over his ass to make sure he recovered from that gunshot wound. And then, I figured, they were so happy to have three squares, a roof over their head, and their precious Jules still alive, they didn't bust my chops, but instead followed my rules and did as told.

Roam didn't openly rebel. Roam was more man than most grown men I'd known by the time I got him at fifteen. Definitely now. He did his chores with no backtalk, and now he did them without me even asking. Ditto with his schoolwork. He didn't mouth off. And he was smart enough not to let me catch him eating Doritos when he knew I'd want him to eat a banana.

Sniff mostly did the same.

Except in times like this.

I'd always wondered about times like this.

But I'd never asked.

Now, I asked.

"Are you just bein' a teenage boy or are you rebelling against authority?"

"Isn't that one and the same?" he asked back.

I added one more choice. "Or is it that you're just a smartass?"

"That last one," Roam answered for Sniff, coming in from outside where he'd been firing up the grill.

He already had the spatula in his hand even if no meat was over the heat.

My boy was on a mission.

I stared at him as he sauntered into the kitchen, all long legs, loose hips, eighteen and entirely in control of his own body.

And so handsome.

Lord.

He was beautiful.

I looked at Sniff.

He'd put away the Doritos but now his hand was on the side of the deep fryer, checking the temperature even though the light went off to tell us when it was ready and that light was still on.

He got all As.

Didn't even try. Studied, but didn't like it much so did the least he could.

I wondered what he'd do if he'd try.

I wondered if he'd be a doctor or an engineer or an architect.

But I knew in my bones, whatever he wanted, he'd be able to do it.

Roam got As too, but some Bs. He was a reader. He got math and science stuff that was way beyond me.

But he had no patience for writing. English Comp irritated the hell out of him. And if he had a report to write, Lordy. *Watch out.* That put my boy in a *mood*.

But they were so much more than good-looking.

So much more than sharp.

Smart.

They were funny.

They were loyal.

They were mine.

Right then, in my kitchen, it was not the first time I wondered about their parents, even if I knew the greatest penance they could endure was never knowing the men they'd made.

Never knowing how beautiful those two boys turned out.

Never knowing the goodness they put on this earth.

And worst of all, not caring.

But that was what I was thinking right then in my kitchen.

Somehow, some way, I got the chance to know all that.

Feed it.

Nurture it.

Hold it in my heart.

"Sniff," I whispered.

"Yeah, Shirleen," he answered the deep fat fryer.

"I love you, boy."

His body shot straight and turned to me.

I felt the air in the room go electric.

I also felt Roam's attention hone in on me.

So I looked to him.

Right in the eye.

"I love you too, Roam. You're the best thing to ever happen to me. In my entire life." I included Sniff in my look. "Both you boys. Blessings. I can count my blessings on two fingers. But they're the best ones I coulda ever got."

"You okay, Shirleen?" Roam asked quietly.

"You're in my kitchen, son, and so's your brother. So yeah. I'm the best I've ever been," I replied.

Sniff looked to Roam.

Roam didn't take his eyes off me.

Sniff stopped looking at Roam and moved my way, muttering, "Gonna hit the shower real quick before dinner."

But as he was about to walk by me, he leaned in and down and kissed my cheek.

Then he hit the stairs to the basement where both the boys had their big TV room and bedrooms.

Roam just went to the fridge, got the platter of burger patties, closed the fridge and walked right by me to the doors to the outside.

He stopped inside them after he'd opened one.

And he turned to me.

"You know we love you too, yeah?" he asked.

I clenched my teeth together real hard and nodded.

"Yeah," he said and walked out the door, sliding it closed behind him.

I watched through the windows as he moved to the grill, plate of burgers in one hand, grill spatula in the other.

I wasn't sure I'd saved them.

Jules was on a mission to do that before I came into the picture.

But I had a hand in that.

A good strong hand.

God gave me that shot.

So maybe He hadn't given up on me.

Maybe He believed in me enough to give me a second chance.

And then, when I refused to let Him down...

Upon me He bestowed His blessings.

SIX

WONDERS

Shirleen

The next night, as the Uber came to a stop at the curb in front of the walk up to Moses's front door, I checked out his place.

Newish build. Three stories. Attached on both sides to other units. Since we drove by the alley that ran behind his place, I knew the bottom floor was the garage, so the top two floors had to be the living area. The trees around the development had not filled in yet.

Still, it was nice. Neat. Attractive.

And Moses had some big pots on his front porch, already filled with flowers.

I started up the walk as the Uber driver took off and Moses's front door opened.

He leaned against the jamb.

Okay, changed my mind.

His house was *da bomb*.

His eyes weren't on me.

They were watching the Uber take off.

"Hey," I called.

His gaze slowly came to me. "Hey."

He didn't move from his door as I took the two steps up his stoop, off of which was his cute little porch with its flower pots, which also had two red Adirondack chairs on it with a table in between.

Seeing as he was in my way and not moving, I stopped.

"Something wrong with your car?" he asked.

"I hope not, since Roam's out on a date in it."

"Something wrong with your phone?"

I was confused but I answered, "No."

"So is there some reason you didn't use it to phone and ask me to pick you up?"

Ah.

"It's all good, my man," I assured. "I'm an Uber expert."

"Sniff at home?" he asked, not moving from barring me from his house.

"No. He's out with some buds," I answered.

"So it isn't that you didn't want him to catch me picking you up."

Hmm.

"Moses."

"Okay. Before we start this date, since I got your undivided attention, I'll share something important. You've been an independent woman a long time. Lookin' out for yourself. Lookin' out for your boys. I get that's habit. And I'll point out I find it attractive. But we do this, it works with you and me, you will no longer be alone. You'll have someone to help look out for you. Granted, you'll have someone else to look out for, but he'll be returning that favor. To end, if you need a ride, *you call*."

If I was a normal Rock Chick, say, any one of them but Daisy, I would lose my mind at him barring the door to deliver this statement, a statement not even vaguely disguised as a command. I'd then stomp off and call my girls to meet me at a bar so I could throw a hissy fit.

I was not a normal Rock Chick.

I was me.

So I said, "Okay."

"Okay, baby," he whispered then moved aside so I could enter his house.

I walked in, deciding not to hide I was interested in what I was seeing.

Up front, carpeted stairs that were nice.

To the right, a door that opened to what was clearly a laundry/storage room, what with the telltale signs of washer and dryer and bikes mounted on the wall.

I headed up the steps.

There was a landing where things got interesting, this being a little alcove cut out of the pearly-white wall. There was an African tribal mask on a stand set there, lit from above. It was beat up a little, but painstakingly painted, and still had all the little shells that ran across the top.

"Nice," I noted, stopping to look at it.

"*Ngady amwaash.* Mask for a woman. From the Congo."

I looked up at him. "No kidding?"

"My uncle was a collector of African art. On our twenty-first birthdays, he gave all his kids and nieces and nephews a piece." He tipped his head to the mask. "That was mine."

I looked down at it. "It's amazing."

"Yep."

"I should do something like that for Roam," I murmured.

"Yep."

I looked at him again to see he was grinning at me.

He then put his hand to the small of my back and propelled me up the next flight of stairs.

More nice.

Wood floors.

A living room to the left, big.

A kitchen to the right, also big, off which there was a bar and beyond that a dining room table.

Balconies off the front and back.

I didn't know what was behind it, but between living room and kitchen there was a big pantry, the doors were open and inside it was a work of art.

"Don't get ideas," Moses said as I stared at it. The distressed wood countertop that had been installed into it. The drawers under it with interesting handles, the cabinets under the drawers that had dense wire mesh as fronts. The shelves above it a display of pantry-type items in baskets, jars and glass canisters as well as cans on recessed baby shelves. All of it could be photographed for a magazine. "I let my oldest loose on that. I made it. She designed it. And after her week is up with her mom, she comes back and straightens it when I fuck everything up."

I again turned my gaze to him. "She's got an eye."

"She wants to be an interior designer, and the rest of the house will reflect her desire to do that."

I smiled at him.

He took that opportunity to lean in and touch his lips to mine.

Oowee.

When he pulled back, I tried to keep breathing right as I remarked, "It's sweet, you let her loose."

"Let her loose as much as I can. She's got an eye, a talent, and will need clients who do not have the limited budget her old dad has. Fortunately, she looks at it as a challenge." His gaze roamed my face before he looked back into my eyes and asked, "You hungry?"

I nodded.

Hand to my waist, he propelled me into his kitchen, saying, "Let's get you fed."

Interesting punched tin backsplash above the stove. Gray concrete countertops. Stainless steel appliances. His girl took into account her dad was a guy in everything but the stained glass suncatcher hanging in the window shaped like a sunflower.

"You wanna sit in front of the TV and eat or you wanna eat at the bar and talk first?" Moses asked, getting down plates.

"Bar," I answered. "Can I help?"

"Next time, yeah. This time, let me look after you. Have a seat at the bar, baby. Wine to drink? Or beer."

"Wine's good," I told him, heading around to the wooden stools on the other side of the bar.

He got down a wineglass as I hefted my ass up on a stool.

"Red or white?" he asked.

"You got both?" I was surprised. He drank beer all through dinner at Barolo Grill.

He looked to me. "You were coming over. So yeah, I got both."

I didn't know what to say to that because I didn't know what to think.

Leon had put some effort into it in the beginning, but not much. I was too young. I didn't know to expect more, expect better. And by the end I suspected even in the beginning he had no clue how to give more, definitely not better.

I'd never had a man serve up a meal to me unless I was paying him as a waiter at a restaurant.

Or buy me wine.

"Red," I said softly.

His head tipped to the side and his attention became acute. "You good?"

I had kind, decent, loving friends. I had a job I was proud of. I had two boys under my roof I wasn't quite done raising, and I didn't get to them until late, but what I'd done, I'd done right.

And I was on a stool in Moses Richardson's kitchen.

What I was not was "good."

There was no definition for the wonder I was feeling.

"Yeah," I replied.

He studied me a beat, nodded, then moved to a bottle of red wine on his counter.

Moses was opening it when he asked, "There a reason why those boys don't have their own cars?"

"I made a mistake."

He pulled out the cork, but didn't move to fill my glass, just looked at me.

I took that to mean "explain."

I explained.

"In the beginning, I wanted them to trust me. But I was stuck. They'd been gettin' on on their own for a while, they didn't need me to feed them and give them a bed. Still, beds and food at my place were better than what they could scrounge up. Their clothes were for shit. Secondhand, got 'em at the shelter. They had phones and I did not ask how they got them, or how they paid for them, but they weren't top of the line."

When I paused, Moses nodded to tell me he was with me.

So I kept going.

"Coulda gone the route of givin' them everything they needed and most of what they wanted. But I didn't think spoiling them was the way to make them trust me and the home I was giving them. Bought them enough they had new of what they needed, got 'em good phones and I paid for the plan. But that was it. Otherwise, I gave 'em chores so they'd get allowances and have money in their pockets to buy themselves things. I didn't want to just hand everything over so they didn't learn how to work for something they wanted. It was more, though. I wanted it normal. I wanted to teach things and for them not to expect things. But I also wanted them to know I wasn't buying them or their behavior or my place in their hearts."

"Think that was a smart move, sweetheart," Moses said, now pouring my wine.

"Yeah, the problem with it was, they never asked for anything. Not once. Not new jeans. Not new phones. Not new undies. Not a thing. Christmas is crisis time for Shirleen. Got no clue what they want or need." I shook my head. "But anyway, got it in my head cars were too big a deal for them. Especially two boys who'd had nothing, until they got me. They'd definitely never ask. I couldn't just hand them over, 'cause what am I teachin' 'em if I did? So I decided, anytime they wanted the Navigator, I'd give it to 'em. And told 'em, they both graduated high school on the honor roll, they could pick their own cars. That way, they'd earn 'em. But I didn't realize I'd be putting myself on the Uber VIP list for frequent riders by doing all of that."

Moses set my wineglass in front of me. "Since they're graduating soon, you won't have to worry about it much longer. Unless they're not on the honor roll."

"They're on the honor roll," I shared, lifting the glass and taking a sip.

Nice. Dry. But fruity. With a hint of oak.

The man could pick wine.

Maybe he *was* perfect.

"Two street kids graduating on the honor roll," he murmured, pulling a bag of big sesame seed buns his way. "You're like a miracle worker."

"They're smart kids. They don't even try. It just happens," I told him.

He turned his eyes to me. "They gotta go to class. They gotta pay attention in class. They gotta hand in assignments, which means they gotta do homework. And they gotta pass tests, which means they gotta study at least a little bit. So no, Shirleen, that shit doesn't 'just happen.' Kids do that because they're either taught to do it because they've lived lives with parents that helped them learn to live those lives right. Or because they respect the person who's lookin' after them and they don't want to let her down."

"I hear that, honey," I said softly and watched his eyes flare. I didn't get the flare, but I kept on the current subject. "What I'm sayin' is, they're good kids. Smart kids. And that's just how they are, natural-like. I didn't make that in them. That's who they are. So I don't think I should get credit for that. I think they have to understand who they are and it's good down deep so they don't ever get it into their heads that what made them is what *is* them, because it's not. They're their own people and *they* built that through hard work and just bein' good."

He pulled the top off a Crock-Pot, after which zesty, saucy goodness wafted into the room, doing this saying, "This is because you're humble."

"Roam took a bullet for Jules."

He stopped spooning brisket on the bottom of a bun and turned to me.

"And one of the reasons Roam and Jules didn't die on the floor of that living room is because Sniff was runnin' flat out, he'd lost his phone, so he was flagging down anyone who would stop, lookin' for help. Just God's love that the car he flagged down had Luke Stark in it."

"Sweetheart," he whispered.

"What made them is there, natural-like," I said firmly.

"Okay, baby," he agreed quietly.

Since we had that straight, I took a sip of wine.

He dished up, and when he slid my plate in front of me, it did not have a sandwich and some chips on it.

It had a sandwich, potato salad, a mound of spinach salad with bacon, blue cheese crumbles and red onion sliced so thin you could see through it (and thank God I had mints in my bag for that) and baked beans he pulled out of the oven in a crock he had to have gotten from his momma.

"You wanna feed me or make me explode?" I asked as I stared down at my plate.

"My momma taught me, worst thing a guest could do after they sit at your table is want for more and not be able to get it. She never laid a table where each serving dish wasn't filled to the brim with more in the kitchen."

"And you took that one giant leap further and put so much on a plate a woman can't get through it."

He slid his ass up on the stool beside mine and grinned at me. "You complaining?"

I pointed a fork at my plate. "Is there molasses in these beans?"

"Brown sugar. I came home at lunch and started them up. They've been cookin' for five hours."

Nice.

"No, I'm absolutely not complaining," I belatedly answered.

He leaned into me and gave me another lip touch (which was good, pre-blue cheese and onions) before he turned to his own food.

He was scooping up some potato salad mixed with beans (I approved) when I called, "Moses."

He turned his head my way.

"No man has ever come home at lunch to make up some beans for me."

Warmth (or more accurately, *more* warmth) seeped into his eyes. "Hate you had to wait this long, but still honored to be the first."

"Stop bein' perfect," I whispered.

"Gonna stretch that out, Shirleen, as long as I can."

It was then I leaned in and gave Moses a lip touch.

I didn't look at his face as I sat back and turned to my food.

The beans were sublime.

The brisket was orgasmic.

But it was the company that altered my world.

I WOULD FIND, around about the time all was well in the world of Tarzan and Jane, that making out on the couch like teenagers, hot and heavy, was a skill that stood the test of time, even if you didn't practice it.

And I would find, to my horror, that post-traumatic stress was not just for soldiers.

This I would find when Moses was deftly sliding into second base, hand inching toward my breast.

I wanted him to tag that bag more than I wanted my next breath.

And then my mind blanked, sheer panic saturated every cell in my body, and somehow I was off my back on the couch with Moses's long length on top of me.

Instead I was across the room, breathing hard, hand up his way like I was fending him off even as he lay on his side on the couch, up on a forearm, his breathing also accelerated, his eyes alert and locked on me.

"Baby," he whispered cautiously.

I still felt the tingle in my lady parts, the taste of him in my mouth, the feel of his heat against my skin, the weight of him on my body.

I could see his beauty right there on his couch.

But my brain was twisting shit up, feelings I was feeling making him grow foggy.

I wasn't having visions, seeing Leon's ghostly face hovering over the magnificence that was Moses.

It was all in the emotions as things I hadn't felt in years started stomping through the dust in my bones, kicking it up, making me not able to see straight.

"Shirleen," Moses called, slowly moving his body so he was seated on the couch before, equally slowly, straightening from it.

Okay.

All right.

This was movie night with Moses.

This was brisket and baked beans, and lip touches and smiles and good wine while he told me about his oldest, Judith, named after his momma, spending an entire summer in search of the perfect lamps for his nightstands. She had this mission because, after he'd recovered from the financial strain of the divorce and the ensuing legal battles, three years ago he'd moved his daughters into this place and had given his eldest a budget to do her dad's pad up right. And even at fourteen, she apparently took this task seriously.

He also told how he was struggling with what it said about him that he had a problem with her latest boyfriend, who was white "when I never saw my girl with anything but a brother."

And he shared about his youngest, Alice, named after her momma's favorite writer, Alice Walker, and how she was a good kid, a great one. But she'd arranged three sit-ins that year on a variety of things that she wanted changed about the school and "she just cares about things so much, baby. She wants change yesterday, doesn't understand she can't have it and I'm worried what the world is gonna do to my little girl when she realizes it's never gonna be easy, it's always gonna be hard and sometimes impossible."

In other words, dinner was not light. It was heavy and it was the sweetest conversation I'd had, because he trusted me with these things about his girls, about his feelings about his girls, and that was an honor the likes I'd never had bestowed on me.

Tarzan, as fantastic as it was, was a letdown after that. But we needed light after all that heavy and it was good to cuddle through a movie with a man. Hear his beautiful chuckle. Feel his arms around me. Smell his scent. Be in his space.

And kissing after the movie was over was a revelation. I couldn't say it started out easy, I was stiff. The ease came later as Moses led me to it, and he made it good before it got *good*.

Now I was there.

Across the room facing off with a decent, kind, deep-feeling man who could cook brisket and pick wine while the dust of the one from before drifted up in my bones, blinding me and making my mouth feel dry.

"Talk to me," he urged.

"I...this...I...this," I stuttered then shook my head. "This isn't gonna work."

"She cheated on me."

I blinked at him when these words came at me.

"Sorry?" I asked.

"At her high school reunion. With her high school boyfriend. She got drunk off her ass and cheated on me."

He was talking about his wife.

Had to be.

And was she insane?

I'd only had his kisses.

And they were fabulous.

But I'd also had a good amount of what else made him.

So she had to be insane.

"I—"

He cut me off.

"Kept talkin' to him on the phone after. Believe her when she says it didn't go further than the reunion physically. But she kept contact. Even after I found out and we got into counseling. She ended it with him only while we were in counseling. But I heard her talking to him, tellin' him to quit calling, and when I confronted her with it, she admitted she kept that up for a while. Needed it somehow. But it was over. He just wouldn't quit calling."

"I'm sorry, Moses."

He nodded his head sharply, only once.

"I am too. I loved her. And I gotta take responsibility for my fuckup, because I perpetrated one. I was a man and acted like a dumb-shit man. We had babies and I helped her make them and then I did my thing. Went to work. Went to the gym. Might go to the grocery store but other than that, pretty much expected her to do everything. Feed 'em. Bathe 'em. Get 'em to bed. Take care of the house. I spent time with my babies, of course, they were my babies. I'd do the odd thing here or there to pitch in. But mostly I took the good times. Not the waking-up-in-the-middle-of-the-night times. The tough stuff, I was gone. Mostly at work. Could say I needed the overtime, I worked hard, and everyone can use more money. But truth was, I loved my job, so it wasn't that. I was just doin' whatever I wanted to do. She had a job too. Two of them, one bein' a momma, one in an office. She was worn out. She was also fed up with it."

"I, yes...I mean, I don't know, but I think that wouldn't be much fun," I murmured.

"The thing was, she didn't say dick about it. Not until counseling. So I saw the error of my ways after the fact. And I was good to hold up my hand and cop to it. Even could see, just a little, not totally, but enough to maybe forgive her for having a weak moment, getting hammered and thinking, what if? What if it had worked out with that guy back in high school? What would her life be like if she wasn't raisin' two girls mostly on her own with her husband MIA at work? I could also see wanting to go back in time when it was simpler. When there wasn't the house, the husband, the kids, the job. When it was just dressin' up, goin' out, booze and fucking and good times."

I nodded.

I mean, I wasn't sure I agreed with him. That was a leap to take and said a lot about him that he'd try to find a way to forgive a disloyalty of that magnitude. That he'd try to understand what lay beneath it.

But it wasn't my experience, my marriage, my spouse, so it wasn't my call to make.

For my part, Leon cheated on me all the time.

And when he did, I just found it a relief.

Moses kept speaking.

"Talkin' to him, though, that I didn't get. She betrayed our love, me, our vows, and I agreed to try to work that shit out, and every phone conversation from the first after she got back from that reunion, to the last when I caught her tellin' him to stop phonin' was another betrayal. Why didn't she tell me he was calling? Why didn't she just hang up? And every time her phone rang from then on, was I gonna think it was him or some other guy she was asking 'what if?'"

"I can see that," I said quietly.

"She told me in counseling that maybe she needed the attention. To feel attractive. To feel wanted. By that time, it was flowers for no reason and me breakin' my back to prove I was doin' my part for our family and regular date nights to keep the us in our marriage. So I did not get why she needed another man's attention when outside of what I was giving my girls, she had all of mine."

Seemed to me she was a selfish bitch.

I did not share this.

"So I called bullshit," he declared.

"I can see that too," I replied.

And I really could.

"Is that enough to end a marriage, break apart a family?" he asked.

"I don't know, darlin'," I answered.

"I didn't either. What I knew was, after I lost my shit when I found out my wife fucked another man, I got myself together. About that. But those phone calls jacked with my head. I could deal with a one-time thing. A wakeup call for us both. We were on the wrong path and that wasn't the way to yank us back to the right one, but shit happens. But those fuckin' calls, Shirleen, all I could think was not about those calls or even about her needing attention. Once I knew he was still phoning, anytime I thought about a call, all I could think about was him inside my wife. Blinded by it. Pissed as hell at it. Couldn't get it out of my head. And the question became, should I sacrifice my peace of mind for my children, and worse, teach them if, God forbid, they find themselves in the same situation, that they should swallow betrayal and live on the edge with distrust clouding every moment, and in the end give up any chance of true happiness?"

"I can't answer that for you, Moses."

"Well I could, after she nearly bankrupted me taking me to court repeatedly to teach me a lesson about how she feels when she doesn't get what she wants, using our daughters as tools to do that. I couldn't imagine the woman I married had that in her. But she did. So I got my answer. And so did our daughters, watching their mother put their father through that. Don't think it was the man she met that made her stop. I think it was the fact her daughters were drifting away, angry at her for making shit ugly. That's what made her stop."

"I'm glad something did," I told him.

"Me too."

When he said no more, I asked carefully, "How are things now? I mean, you said at the grocery store that you two had it together, but—"

"I can barely stand to look at her."

Oh boy.

"*That*," he went on, "I do for my daughters when school functions mean I have to be in her space. And don't take that anger at her as me still having feelings for her. I don't. That anger is not about what she did to me, to us, but what she did to my girls. No one fucks with my girls, and for four years I had no choice but to put up with my wife fucking with our girls."

Yep.

A selfish bitch.

"Other than school functions," he continued, "we do not have one of those arrangements where we share Christmas Eve dinner or I come to her family's big Fourth of July parties. There's my house, our family, and there's their mother's house and the family they got with her."

To that, I had no choice but to utter an understatement.

"That's very sad."

"Do I deserve that for bein' a man and bein' clueless and makin' babies with my wife and not pitchin' in?"

I shook my head. "I...I don't think so. I mean, she should have said something."

"Yeah. She should have. We didn't start our family young. We were both in our thirties. Our friends had kids. Both our families are in town. We're both tight with them. We weren't immature and finding our way on our own. And we'd been together a long time. She knew how to communicate with me."

I nodded that I heard him.

"I still fucked up. That was on me. Sayin' what I just said, it was me who was old enough to know better than to make babies with my wife and not take care of all of them. And I didn't."

"I don't want to, you know, butt in here and defend you when all you've shared is all I know about the situation. I wasn't around and I've never met the woman. But even though that really was not good,

Moses, with what happened I think it's safe to say something would have happened anyway."

"Yeah," he agreed. "Though easy for me to think that because it makes me the good guy in the end no matter how you look at it."

I just gave him big eyes because that was true.

Still, the woman stepped out on him rather than telling him to step up then she took out her anger at him using their daughters.

She had it in her to fuck their shit up.

And that was going to happen, one way or another.

I'd pretty much said this already, therefore I didn't repeat it.

"So there it is," he stated.

"Yes," I agreed. "There it, um...is."

"Your turn."

My throat closed and I felt my joints seize.

Moses didn't miss anything and I knew he didn't miss any of that.

He still didn't let up.

"What'd he do to you?"

I didn't see this coming. Tit for tat. He laid it out, made himself vulnerable, showing me the way, making it safe to follow.

I still didn't want to take that way.

"I think—" I began.

"Baby, you look good and you dress good and you kiss good and you listen good and you open up good." He lifted a hand and gestured between us. "I want this. I want more. I want to know more about you and eventually I'll want to be inside you."

Oh God.

"This is too fast," I told him. "Too fast and too soon."

"Five minutes ago this wasn't going to work. Now I can go slow. But I cannot have you preparing to bolt every time something tweaks you. Preparing to bolt *and* ready to end us. I need you to *talk to me*."

His ex had not talked to him and his whole life got derailed.

Damn.

I shook my head but said, "I don't know what happened. He's just *in there*."

"How?"

"In my bones. In my soul. It was all good and then it wasn't and I was across the room and I don't even know how I got here. I just know he was back."

"He's dead."

"Not in a way he'll ever be gone."

"Dead is dead, sweetheart, it's *you* who can control if he stays alive the ways he can."

"He beat me."

It was like he'd crossed the room, wrapped his hand around my throat and squeezed so I couldn't take a breath, the anger burning from him was so strong, the air in the room vanished.

"I did not enjoy having sex with him. He did not care. He took what he wanted whenever he wanted."

I'd felt the room.

Why did I say more?

Now his arms were bent at his sides, his fingers curled into fists, his chest moving steady but fast, the heaves powerful, rhythmically lifting his entire torso as his eyes stayed glued to me.

"I'm too much for you, or any man, to take on," I whispered.

"You wet for me?" he growled.

"S-say what?"

"Are. You. *Wet*. For me?"

Oh Lordy.

Just him asking that question made me wet(ter) for him even if we were having a serious conversation that shouldn't be sexy at all.

It was jerky but I nodded my head.

"You were there with me, *definitely* there with me, I was about to take it further, and then you were across the room. What triggered that?"

"I don't know. It just happened."

"Something triggered it, baby."

I shook my head.

"No one since him?" he asked, going for gentle, I could tell. It was still slightly terse because he was still highly pissed after I shared what Leon had done to me.

"I...yes, but none that mattered."

"I matter."

I closed my eyes so tight I felt the wrinkles in my lids.

Because this was oh so true.

"That's it. I matter," he said to me. "And you're either scared you're gonna fuck this up or you're scared you're not reading it right and you'll find you've picked another asshole."

I opened my eyes.

"I'm not sure I have it in me to give you what you deserve," I admitted.

"And what's that?"

"Goodness. No drama. Just a clean go without history and piles of shit you got to wade through to maybe make it to the other side, but that result is not guaranteed because there's so much shit, you might find you need to give up for your own sake."

"You think I'm gonna give up on you?" he asked, a tad bit scarily.

"I don't know. More, I'm not sure I'm worth the effort."

The air evacuated the room again because he was pissed as shit again.

I decided maybe it was best if I stopped talking.

"I thought we got past this," Moses said when I said nothing.

"You don't see."

"Make me see."

Suddenly I threw up both hands at my sides.

"It wasn't what Leon did to me, Moses!" I snapped. "He was always good for nothin'. And I let him have me. What does that say about me?"

"I don't know, but obviously you do, so I want to hear you say it."

"My sister, Dorothea, she was the pretty one. She was the quiet one. She was the sweet one. She got the handsome man. She made the beautiful family."

"And that wasn't for you?"

"I was the hell raiser. I was good for nothin', just like Leon."

"So you had sass and that means you didn't deserve a good life with a decent man in it?"

"I was never good enough."

"Good enough for what, Shirleen? Good enough for who?"

"Good enough for my teachers, who thought I was slow. Good enough for my father, who took off on us. Good enough for my aunts and uncles, who saw a hellion and thought I'd never amount to anything."

"So you proved them right."

I lifted my chin. "Damn straight."

"And then you had time enough without their bullshit, and with your husband dead and not beating you or raping you to realize who you were and you proved them wrong. 'Cause you know, baby, you know a man takes you without you wanting him to, he's your husband or not, it's rape."

My teeth clacked audibly I shut my mouth so fast.

"I don't know who you were, sweetheart," he continued. "But every day I see kids who someone doesn't think will amount to much and even if that shit is not right, they're convinced of it just because the asshole adults around them feel the need to share. And you know what?"

"What?" I whispered.

"In most cases, it's got fuck all to do with the kid. It's about the asshole adult feelin' less, understanding their limits, and the kid's got smarts or spirit or a big personality or a sweet disposition, and they gotta do what they gotta do to shut that down because they're jealous as fuck and they know deep inside they'll feel even smaller than they already are because that kid is gonna be something. So they not only gotta drag the kid down, they gotta smother the life out of them."

Suddenly, I was breathing funny.

"Half the problems in Gilliam are kids with parents who don't give that first fuck, or who are so messed up it's a miracle they can get themselves out of bed in the morning, and some don't even try," he bit off. "The other half are kids with parents or adults in their lives who are determined to do one thing in their miserable lives and that's finding a way to make damn sure that child doesn't show them up by making something of themselves when they didn't have what it took to do the same thing. You know that shit people say where a kid is just misunderstood?"

I nodded.

"Well in a lot of cases, that shit is right. It is very rare when a kid is just a bad seed. For the most part, someone planted that seed and put a lot of effort into forcing it to grow and in a kid, that ground is fertile. It's so much easier to think bad of ourselves than it is to think good. And that shit blooms fast and out of control."

"I had a good momma, Moses. A good family. Not a good daddy, but the rest? They didn't deserve what I did to them."

"If they made you feel less, Shirleen, then they got what they made. It's the woman standing across from me right now that *you* made and that has nothing to do with them."

"I love that you think that way but—"

"*Fuck, baby!*" he exploded, tossing both his arms wide and leaning toward me even as his outburst shocked me so much I leaned back. "Do you not think I see young Shirleens every day of my life? Do you not understand that I know more than maybe anybody how hard it is to pull yourself free of the shit you let yourself get bogged under and find your way clean? Do *you* not get how huge what you've done is?"

"He lives in me," I said weakly.

"You let him," he clipped.

"Everything you do, I compare to what he did."

He leaned back and crossed his arms on his chest. "Well, shit, sweetheart. You're human. You had a man who did you wrong and you found a man you like that you might want in your life, so you're comparing the old with the new so you can make sure you don't fuck up again. I'm not sure I can cope with you bein' smart and lookin' out for yourself so you don't make the same mistake twice. Best get on calling Uber so you can take your sweet ass and your common sense home."

At that speech, I couldn't stop myself from cracking a smile.

His eyes narrowed. "You find something funny?"

"Well, uh...yeah."

He uncrossed his arms and planted his hands on his hips before he rumbled warningly, "I'm not bein' funny, baby."

I decided to shut up again.

"In time, you will learn I'm not him," he said low.

"Okay," I whispered.

"Now I told you we'd go slow and you may have forgotten that, so I'll remind you, Shirleen, this is at your pace. As long as we're movin' forward, I'm good. So next time I take shit too far, you don't bolt out of my arms and hold up your hand to me like I'm causin' you harm. You say, 'Moses, honey, I need you to slow down,' and that will happen. I swear it."

My God.

I could fall in love with this man.

No.

Damn.

I *was* falling in love with him.

"Shirleen, you hear me?" he prompted when I said nothing.

"I hear you, honey."

"And you are not fuckin' Ubering home."

I nodded.

"Your boys won't be watchin' for you, will they?"

I shook my head.

"Good," he muttered.

"Are we done making out?" I asked.

"I don't know, are we?" he asked back.

I pressed my lips together, tight.

"Get over here, woman," he ordered.

My breath caught.

I'd heard one of the Hot Bunch demand that of one of his Rock

Chick so many times, I'd be able to buy Roam and Sniff top of the line Mercedes if I had a dollar for every time I heard it.

And I always just shook my head, sometimes mentally, sometimes physically, thinking if I had a man who told me to walk my ass to him, I'd walk my ass the other way.

That man being Moses, I walked my ass right to him.

He wrapped his arms loose around me.

I placed my hands on his chest.

They felt good there.

Under my right one, I could feel his heart beating, strong and true.

"You gonna read me the riot act every time I freak out?" I asked.

"Only when the situation warrants it," he answered.

Hmm.

"I'm gonna be some work," I told him something he couldn't have missed.

He confirmed my suspicion by saying, "I didn't miss that."

I slid a hand up and curled my fingers around the side of his neck.

His arms grew tighter.

"I don't want you to think I didn't love him. For some reason, that's important to me. In my way, the girl I was, not yet a woman, I loved him," I admitted.

"Okay, baby," he whispered.

"Before I hated him," I finished.

He nodded before he dipped his head, his cheekbone brushing against mine as he pulled me even closer to give me a hug.

A hug.

He held me to him in his living room like he intended to do that all night.

And I could stand there all night.

I could stand there for weeks, held in Moses Richardson's arms.

Eventually, he asked, "You want ice cream?"

"Yeah."

He lifted his head and looked in my eyes. "You wanna make out some more before, after or in the middle of ice cream?"

I shot him a grin. "All of the above."

He grinned back.

When he dipped his head that time, it was to capture my mouth.

He kissed me soft before he slid his tongue inside.

I wrapped my arms around his neck and pressed against him.

He angled his head and took the kiss deep.

I cupped the back of his head with a hand to hold him right where he was.

It didn't feel good being held to him like this, feeling his strength pressed against me, his tongue stroking mine leisurely, taking it slow, giving, sweet.

The wonders of all that had no words to describe them.

And I lost myself to whatever that was.

Since I was lost, happy where I was, in his embrace, connected to him, Moses gave me all I was willing to take.

He did scoop out some ice cream for us.

He just did it…

Later.

SEVEN

CHOICES

Shirleen

Afternoon the next day, I was sitting in my Navigator, staring at the high school, my phone in my hand, my heart in my throat.

This was because Roam's history teacher had called and asked me to come in to have "a discussion."

I hated schools. I'd take visiting a hospital or walking my ass into a police station over walking into a school.

And with my old profession, both of those were saying something.

Not to mention, with my membership in the Rock Chicks, being able to visit a hospital or walk into a police station was an important skill to have.

Moses told me he often didn't have his phone on him when he was at work.

Still, for whatever reason, I pulled up his text string, which had seven texts (yes, I counted). Him giving me his address. Me confirming I got it. Him saying something sweet after I confirmed. Me telling him I was on my way to his house last night. Him confirming he got that and telling me he was looking forward to feeding me. Me texting that morning to say I'd had a good time the night before. Him replying, telling me he did too.

I'm at the school. Roam's teacher called. I'm worried, I typed in.

Neither boy had had trouble with school. It took some tutoring to get them up to scratch when they started back after being out for so long, but then they just assimilated.

Easy as pie.

Which freaked me out.

I'd talked to Jules about it because I'd found that odd. I thought that would be a battle too and was surprised when it wasn't.

"We'll keep an eye, Shirleen," she'd said. "But not for the normal reasons. Sometimes, when kids get it good after they've had it bad, they try overly hard to prove they deserve to have something that's just their due. Like an education. They don't want it taken away, so they go beyond the pale to make certain it isn't."

It didn't seem like they were trying overly hard. I didn't have any practice, but it just seemed normal. They didn't have an aversion to school like I did when I was their age. They didn't jump for joy every morning at the prospect of hauling their asses out of bed, shoving their books in their bags and heading out with a pep in their step.

Since it was seemingly normal, we just rolled with it.

And now I'd been called by a teacher to come in "as soon as you can, Miz Jackson," and have "a discussion."

I stared at the text, wondering if I should send it.

In usual circumstances, I might text Daisy, and it wasn't that I wasn't talking to her that I didn't type the text into her string.

It was just...

Now there was Moses.

Before I could chicken out (of a lot of things), I hit send, opened my door, pulled myself out of my car and hoofed it on my high heels to the school.

School was out for the day so the halls were quiet, but I could see through the windows there was a woman at the reception desk in the administration office.

It took a lot, but instead of giving in to my heebie-jeebies I was in a school and turning around to walk right out, I walked in there.

She looked up.

"Hey," I greeted. "I'm Shirleen Jackson. Mr. Robinson called and said he wanted to talk about my boy."

She nodded. "Just out the door, to the left, down the hall, take a right at the end. Mr. Robinson is in the second classroom on the right."

I nodded back, muttered my gratitude and took off, my heels echoing on the tile in the empty hallways, my hackles coming up.

I'd had to have meetings with the folks at school to get the boys admitted. I'd also had to go to parent-teacher conferences for three years running. None of this had been comfortable, and not because I was worried about my street-tough boys in new environs (or not only because of that).

And I was seeing right then it was because it was bringing it all back.

This wasn't just Leon and starting things with him when I was a junior and he was a senior and how bad that all went.

It was that, back then, I hadn't come into me. I was awkward. Uncertain. My older sister was popular, I was not. I hadn't found my way and looking back at it, I'd always felt embarrassed, even humiliated at how I'd handled myself.

But now I saw that there was no way I'd understand who I was, what I wanted and how to get it.

Hell, I wasn't sure I knew any of that now.

But then, I was a kid.

Why did I expect so much of myself?

I found the room and knocked on the open door, my eyes to the handsome, somewhat disheveled man sitting behind the desk.

At my knock, he looked up at me, and I was relieved when he smiled.

"Miz Jackson," he greeted.

"That's me," I answered, taking a step in.

He stood. "Thanks for coming." He gestured to the student desks in front of his own. "Please come in."

I walked in farther as he looked down, shuffled papers around, grabbed some and rounded his desk.

"Have a seat," he invited, and as I took a seat at one of the student desks, he didn't return to his own. He sat at the one beside mine. "We met at parent-teacher conferences last winter."

"I remember," I told him.

"Sorry to take your time, but I thought this was important," he said.

"What was important?" I asked.

He offered the papers he had in his hand to me.

"My students turn in their papers online. I printed this one out. It's Roam's report on the escalation of American involvement in the Vietnam War."

Slowly, I reached out and took it.

When I did, I felt my heart start beating faster because in the top left corner, it said:

Perspectives of American Military Action in Vietnam
American History
Mr. Robinson
By Roam Jackson

Roam *Jackson?*

Roam's last name wasn't Jackson.

Mine was.

"Do you go over your boys' homework, Miz Jackson?" Mr. Robinson asked.

I looked from the papers in my hand to him. "Sometimes. When they ask me."

He dipped his head to the paper. "Did you read that?"

I looked down at it, forcing my eyes to anything but the words ROAM JACKSON.

There were no marks on the paper. No grade.

I read the first couple of lines and saw this was not something Roam had asked me to look over.

I looked back at Roam's teacher and shook my head.

Mr. Robinson nodded his. "Right then. Outside of it being glaringly obvious he did more than watch a couple of episodes of Burns's documentary, a lot more, I'm not entirely certain how to describe the prose of that report."

I felt my back hitch straight. "What are you saying?"

He looked me right in the eye. "It's well beyond a high school senior's aptitude."

That was when I felt my eyes narrow. "You sayin' my boy plagiarized this report?"

He shook his head. "No. I'm saying Roam is an exceptionally gifted and intuitive writer."

Say what?

I stared at him.

"I'm sorry I didn't bring this to your attention before," he went on. "However, even if his earlier reports and test essays were very good, I've noted as the semester wore on, his talent has markedly increased. That said, I've seen nothing from him like that."

"He hates writing reports. It drives him 'round the bend," I said quietly. "Like, *seriously*."

Mr. Robinson nodded. "I'm not surprised. For many outstanding writers, their need to tell their story, get their point across, doing this in the way they want the words to be crafted to share their narrative is a painful process. It can be very frustrating, as they can be very hard on themselves because each word has to be the perfect one and more, they all have to fit just right."

I looked down at the paper.

"It's my understanding Roam hasn't applied to any colleges," Mr. Robinson remarked.

I lifted my gaze again to him. "We had the talk. Only briefly. He didn't seem interested so I didn't push him."

Another nod from Mr. Robinson with a gentle, "I know his history, Miz Jackson, and this doesn't surprise me. Saddens me, but doesn't surprise me. I will say that it's more than just this assignment that made it clear. However with this," he tipped his head to the papers again, "it's more than clear he should go on to higher education."

"To be what?" I asked.

"That's yours," he replied, now pointing at the papers in my hand. "Take it and read it and you'll understand. But I'll tell you what it did for me. That was not a high school report. That was not even a college level essay. When I read that, I forgot I was reading an assignment. It was like I was reading a book, a very good one, and when it was done my first reaction was annoyance because I wanted more."

"Lord," I whispered.

"He took a chance with that, Miz Jackson. He didn't simply inform me of what he'd learned about American involvement in Vietnam. There are four parts to that report told from the perspectives of an American general, a member of the Viet Cong, an American Marine, and a Vietnamese peasant. It reads like fiction even if every word is factually correct. And the even-handed empathy for each viewpoint that he shared through his narrative was astonishing. Especially as written by the hand of a high school senior who wasn't even alive during the conflict he was writing about."

"*Lord*," I breathed.

"Roam is a natural storyteller, Miz Jackson. You can't teach what he's got. His voice is unique, and although I'm not surprised he struggles with it, you will not find even a hint of that in his work. It flows beautifully."

My eyes drifted down to the paper.

"It's too late now to apply for him to start in the fall," Mr. Robinson continued. "But I'd strongly advise you have another discussion with him. With his grades, and the way he writes an essay, he'd have no issues getting accepted and he could perhaps begin for mid-term enrollment. Or he could take some time and start next year."

I didn't see Roam slaving away at a computer, writing books for a living.

I didn't even see him walking around with a backpack on some university campus.

What I saw was the fact my boy's world was opening up.

He had opportunities.

He had choices.

His past was bleak no matter what way you looked at it.

But his future was bright whatever way he wanted to take it.

I didn't feel I had any of that when I sat at a desk like this years ago.

But I got to live it with Roam.

And Sniff.

"Maybe I should have pushed it," I told the papers.

"I wouldn't have," Mr. Robinson told me.

I looked at him.

"It's only a guess," he continued, "but that guess is that you're sensitive to allowing both your boys to feel in control of their lives, their destinies. This is crucial not only because of their pasts, but for them to learn to make smart choices for their futures. It is far from necessary for Roam to have a college degree in order to be a writer, if that's his choice. What's necessary to be a writer is to fill your life with as many experiences as you can get to inform your writing, enrich it. If more schooling is not his thing," he shrugged, "it's not. It isn't everyone's thing. He can gain life experience in a lot of different ways, and I'm sure we can both agree he has more than enough of one kind already. But I'd broach the subject with him again."

"I will, Mr. Robinson."

He smiled. "Please call me Keith."

"And you should call me Shirleen."

His smile got bigger.

I smiled back then looked down at the paper.

"I've been teaching history a long time," he said, and my gaze shifted back to him. "And I have never, not once, assigned a paper when a student has used that kind of creativity in order to fulfill an assignment. I honest to God didn't know how to grade it. I felt like an armchair quarterback who's never played football in his life calling a play."

"Wow," I whispered.

Boy, I couldn't wait to read that report.

"Precisely." He grinned.

"I'll have the talk with him," with *them*, "soon's I can."

"I'm glad to hear it, Shirleen."

I stood. He stood. We shook hands.

And I didn't care what he read in me holding that report to my chest as he walked me to his classroom door.

"Shirleen," he said when we'd reached it.

I stopped just in the hall and turned to him.

"After my mind unboggled, reading that report," he started, "it came to me the young man who wrote it and how that young man got to the point in his life he was in my class and able to write it."

I stared in his eyes.

"They were very lucky to find you," he said quietly.

"I feel it's the other way around," I replied.

He gave me a gentle smile. "Like I said, they were very lucky to find you."

"Gotta admit, Keith, wish I had a teacher like you in high school."

He seemed embarrassed by the compliment, and if he'd scuffed the floor with the toe of his shoe, I would not have been surprised.

"But glad Roam got you," I finished.

"That pleasure has been mine," he returned.

"Like I said, glad Roam got you."

He chuckled and I grinned at him.

We said our goodbyes and I walked a whole lot faster back to my car.

I didn't even start it up after I tossed my bag to the passenger seat before I turned my attention to Roam's report.

I had no idea how long it took me to read.

What I knew when I reached the end was that my boy could seriously *write*.

I was nearly home when my car rang.

I looked down at the dashboard to see it said MOSES CALLING.

I took the call, greeting, "Hey, my man."

"You all right?"

"Yep."

"Roam all right?"

"Apparently, I got Alex Haley livin' under my roof."

"Say again?"

"Just heard the word that Roam's an *exceptionally gifted* storyteller."

"Who gave you this word?"

"His history teacher. And just to say, I just spent the last however many minutes reading Roam's "Perspectives of American Military Action in Vietnam," and the dude does not lie."

Moses chuckled. "So it was good news."

Good?

Hell no.

Exceptionally awesome?

Absolutely.

"We didn't talk much about college. Roam didn't seem into it. Sniff either. I'm opening up discussions again," I shared.

"Good," he murmured.

I let seconds slip by before I whispered, "My boy's *exceptionally gifted*."

"Does this surprise you, baby?" Moses whispered back.

"Not even a little bit." I let more seconds slip by before I asked, "How do I get him to believe it?"

"No idea, sweetheart. But I think the best way to try is just to start."

"I'll be doin' that."

"Good."

I saw my house on the block so I said, "Almost home. Got pride to give and college lectures to speechify."

Another chuckle before, "Call me later, tell me how it goes."

"Will do."

"As you know, girls are back with me tonight. I'll find out their schedules and if there's an opening when they're doin' something else with someone else somewhere else, we'll fill it."

That made me feel warm all over. "Works for me."

"Later, baby. Thanks for sharing this news with me."

I hit the garage door opener. "Thanks for listening to it. Have fun with your girls."

"Will do. 'Bye, sweetheart."

"'Bye, Moses."

We disconnected. I drove into my garage and sat in my car while I hit the door opener again to close it. I didn't get out until the door was down.

Old habits.

I'd barely walked into the house before I heard Sniff shout from the basement, "That you, Shirleen?"

"You better hope so," I shouted back, dumped my Chloe on the kitchen bar, but kept hold of the report as I walked to the steps to the basement.

I went down to see two tall, good-looking boys sprawled on the sectional with game controllers in their hands, attention riveted to the TV and after-school junk consumption evidence all over the coffee table in front of them.

"Pause," I ordered.

Not even a hesitation, they paused the game, then their eyes came to me.

God, my boys were such good boys.

I looked to Roam. "Just got back from rappin' with Mr. Robinson."

His expression shifted from alert to wary but he said not a word.

Sniff, however, as usual, wasn't silent. "Oh shit."

"Apparently," I walked closer to them and tossed the report among the chip bags and cookie packaging on the square coffee table that sat in the middle of the sectional, "you wrote a report he had no clue how to grade."

Roam's gaze dropped to the papers then shot back to me.

"Because it was so good," I finished.

"Whoa," Sniff muttered.

Roam remained silent and stoic.

In the early days, he'd let things through, give things away.

He'd been among the Hot Bunch so long, he'd learned when he wanted to hide something, how to make sure it remained hidden.

It worked my nerves.

But whatever.

I looked between them both. "I'm gonna say this once and I want it heard. Are you both listening to me?"

"Yeah, Shirleen," Sniff answered.

"Yeah," Roam grunted.

"Are you listening good?" I pushed.

"Yeah, Shirleen." Sniff was getting impatient, maybe to get back to his game, probably because he knew a Shirleen Lecture was coming and he wanted it over.

Roam just nodded.

"When I got you, and I knew I was gonna be able to keep you, I set money aside. I didn't know what it was for. Didn't care. Just knew it was for you."

They both stiffened, even Roam.

I kept at them.

"I know you don't ask for anything. Don't expect anything. Maybe don't want anything you can't earn yourself. But that's not how families work. Families look out for each other. And we're family. And I know you two can take care of yourselves, but you gotta give a woman something, and what I want is to give something to you. We had the talk, I didn't push it. We're gonna have it again because I've been informed, Roam, that you got some serious talent with writing. And it didn't escape me with either of you that you get yourself some good grades even if you don't try real hard. So I want you both to think about usin' that money to go to college."

"I'd rather use it to get some wheels," Sniff muttered.

"I'm buyin' you both a car when you graduate," I reminded him.

"I'd rather use it to get some shit-hot wheels," Sniff amended.

"Boy, you don't quit cussin' in front of me, I'm gonna knock you into outer space," I snapped.

Sniff grinned at me.

I rolled my eyes to the ceiling, drew in a breath, let it out, and looked back at them.

"You two can be anything you want to be," I said quietly.

They stiffened again.

I powered through it.

"And I want no limits on that. We don't talk about it and we don't have to, but I'm just gonna say it is not lost on me the limits you've had in your lives and I want you to know, right here, right now, those limits are done. You wanna go to college, it's yours. You don't, that's your choice, but I want you to think real hard on that and know even if it takes a while for you to come to that decision, the resources are there for you to have it. You want something else for your lives, it's your life, you get to make that choice. I'm just sayin' I want you to discuss that with me. Bottom line is, you got choices. There are no limits. I don't care if I'm covering your asses for years of medical school and residency. Your futures include options. Give me the privilege of giving that to you. Don't limit yourselves because you got any concerns at all about taking it."

They said nothing.

"Am I heard?" I asked.

"You're heard, Shirleen," Roam rumbled.

"Yeah, you're heard," Sniff put in.

I looked to Roam. "That report, son, I read it. Nothin' else to say but to share the fact I got so much pride for you, it hurts me inside havin' to contain it and not let it explode all over the place."

"Shirleen," he whispered.

He wasn't hiding anything right then. The goodness coming to me from him came strong and pure.

God, I loved that boy.

Sniff punched his own heart with his fist twice then reached out and punched Roam in the arm with it. "Way to go, my brother."

I loved both of them.

"Piss off," Roam muttered.

And a little bit more eked out.

He was embarrassed.

I fought grinning as I ordered, "Don't tell your brother to piss off."

"He's annoying," Roam returned.

"He's proud of you too," I shot back.

"I totally am," Sniff stated.

Suddenly Roam pushed up from his lounge and clipped, "Shut up."

"Don't tell me to shut up when—" Sniff started.

He stopped talking when Roam pointed in his face then pointed to the ceiling and hissed, "Shut *up*."

Sniff shut up, tensed, then both boys shot off the couch like rockets.

My heart dropped to my feet.

"Stay down here," Roam ordered quietly as he and Sniff swiftly made their way to the stairs.

"What's going on?" I asked.

"Got your phone?" Sniff asked as answer.

"No," I told him.

He dug his phone out of his pocket and tossed it to me.

Oh no.

"Boys," I snapped in a whisper.

Roam was four steps up, Sniff two down from him, when Roam halted and turned to me.

"Stay. Down. Here. And *quiet*," he commanded on his own whisper.

If I wasn't so freaked, I would lament all the time I allowed that boy to hang with the Hot Bunch learning to be so damned bossy.

Instead I was freaked.

Because something was up.

And in the life of the RCHB, something being up could be anything.

I mean, I'd shot a man in my own home because the RCHB (that time it was mostly HB with the RC dragged in) had some big shit going down.

Was I going to let my teenage boys slink, unarmed, up to face uncertain *anything* and wait downstairs for them?

Hell no.

I started to follow when I heard squealed, "Well look at you, sugar bunches of love! You get more handsome each time I see you!"

Daisy.

Daisy had broken into my house.

As fast as my high heels would take me, I stomped up my stairs.

Nope.

Not Daisy.

The Rock Chicks.

Every one of them.

Daisy. Indy. Jet. Roxie. Jules. Ava. Stella. Sadie. Ally. And Annette thrown in, I hoped, for comic relief.

Because we'd need some comedy.

Seeing as I was about to *lose my mind*!

"Did you all break into my house?" I asked furiously.

"Well no, sugar," Daisy answered calmly. "You gave me your key to check on things when you had that staycation that time Vance and Jules took the boys campin' for spring break."

Shit.

"I—" I began.

"Zip it," Ally ordered.

I stared daggers at her and would learn quickly I should not have wasted time staring daggers and instead should have maybe gone for my stun gun when I found myself bum-rushed by ten Rock Chicks through my great room, down my hall, into my bedroom.

"All's good, just Rock Chick business," Jet called behind her to my boys before she slammed the door, turned to rest her back to it and glared at me. "*Two dates* and *no spill?*" she whisper-hissed. "Are you serious?"

"Yeah, I mean, are you *seriously serious?*" Roxie demanded.

I crossed my arms on my chest. "Can't do a freeze out and spill."

"Oh. My. *Goddess!*" Annette screeched. "This room is fuckin' *phat*! I mean, I can see myself...*everywhere.*"

She did a whirl, checking herself out in a variety of directions.

What could I say? It was my bedroom. I decorated in *glamor*.

And glamor meant mirror.

"Annette," Ally clipped.

Annette stopped whirling and grinned at me. "Even your furniture has mirrors. And you got yourself a purple padded headboard. Sah-*weet.*"

"It's lavender," I corrected.

"Whatevs," she replied. "It's *sah-weet!*"

"Can we stop talking about Shirleen's headboard?" Indy asked.

"Unless that headboard's seen some action," Ava added.

"What kinda girl do you think I am?" I asked. "We've only had two dates."

"A healthy, red-blooded one," Ava answered.

"Have you kissed him?" Roxie asked.

"Have you slept with him?" Ally asked.

"What's he look like?" Stella asked.

"Is he tall?" Sadie asked.

"Is he hot?" Indy asked.

"Is he sweet?" Jet asked.

"Are those pillowcases satin?" Annette asked.

"Oh for goodness sake, let her speak," Jules demanded of the Rock Chicks. She looked to me. "By the way, you should know, I know him. In a professional capacity. And I approve."

From Jules, that said a lot. She was a social worker at King's Shelter for kids.

I was still ticked at her because she'd played her part in putting me out there.

"He's tall. He's hot. He's sweet. I've kissed him. I have *not* slept with him," I answered the room at large. "And now you can all just get on out of my house."

Roxie plopped her ass on the low bench at the foot of my bed covered in purply-gray, patterned velvet, declaring, "Shirleen, you cannot be pissed we set you up with a tall, sweet hot guy."

"I can't?" I asked.

"No," she answered immediately.

"Did he really ram his grocery cart into yours at the store?" Sadie queried.

"Yes, he did," I bit off at Sadie.

"Hot," Indy murmured.

"Totally," Ava replied.

"He's a good man. He's a loving man. He's got two daughters he adores. A job that's more a calling. A nice home he let his oldest decorate," I allowed myself to share.

"That's fantastic," Jules said.

"And he could have found out who I was and what I did and excused himself to go to the bathroom and never came back," I finished.

"Oh please," Indy drawled while throwing herself on my bed, totally unpoofing the perfect fold of my duvet.

So I narrowed my eyes at her.

"Like Lee and the boys didn't investigate him to within an inch of his life," she continued.

That was when my eyes, of their own accord, bugged out at her.

"Yeah, and followed him for days," Stella put in.

Say...

What?

"And then Lee had it out with him face to face to make sure it was all good and he wasn't gonna find out about your history and pull a loser move like that," Jet added.

Well, I knew that last part.

"They investigated him?" I asked.

"Of course," Indy answered.

"Does he know this?" I asked.

"Yep. Didn't care. Just wanted to go to dinner with you," Roxie shared.

Good Lord.

He didn't care.

Moses didn't care the Hot Bunch had invaded his privacy, his history.

Followed him.

He just wanted to go out to dinner with me.

I jumped when a pounding came at the door and through it Roam yelled, "Shirleen, you okay?"

"Those boys are *so cute*," Daisy whispered. "They *so* love their Shirleen."

"I'm fine!" I yelled back, hoping he hadn't overheard anything. "And our talk is over. You can go back to playin' your game."

No hesitation before, "You sure?"

"We're her girls!" Daisy shouted. "Of course she's sure. It's just girl talk, sugar bunch! Go on back to your game!"

I gave it a beat until I sensed Roam leaving and turned to Jules. "I had a conversation with his history teacher today. He reported to me Roam's an exceptionally gifted writer."

"Whoa. Wow. Really?" she asked but smiled and said, "Cool," before I could answer.

"I've reopened discussion about college with both of them," I informed her.

Her smile got bigger. "Awesome."

"Uh, as great as it is Roam's exceptionally gifted at something, it's not news, he's a fantastic kid. But we're off hot-guy topic," Ally butted in.

I looked to Ally. "I've said all I'm gonna say."

"You totally have not said all you're gonna say," she shot back.

"Yo, bitch," Annette called, and I looked to my bed to see her standing at my bedside table, the drawer open. "I approve of your choice of vibrator, but you got yourself a hot guy and you don't have any rubbers in here."

Only Annette could get away with snooping through a woman's drawers with said woman right in the room with her.

That was to say she actually couldn't, but she was such a good-natured hippie-chick, you couldn't get mad at her.

"I'll get Lee to buy you some," Indy offered.

My eyes darted to her. "You will *not*."

"Shirleen," Roxie started hesitantly, "perhaps the ship has sailed on pregnancy, but there's more than one reason to use prophylactics."

"I don't need sex education courses at age fifty-three," I snapped at Roxie.

"Then why don't you have condoms?" Jet asked.

"Because Moses hasn't even stepped foot in my house, much less my bedroom," I said to Jet. "And we're not there. We're taking it slow."

There was general vocal merriment to this comment before Ava murmured, "He crashed his grocery cart into hers. They *so* aren't taking it slow."

"Oh my God, we get to do a new pool. I'm in for fifty bucks for Shirleen gettin' the business on her next date," Sadie decreed.

"I see..." Daisy began, tapping a long, French manicured nail that had cherry blossoms painted across it on her lower lip, "date number four."

"Grocery cart ramming, there's no bet here. It's totally going to be the next date," Stella announced. "It's actually a shocker it wasn't the first date."

"Teenage boy blocks," Ava accurately surmised.

I had to stop this even if the famous Rock Chick Getting the Business Pool was started by me so I deserved this ridiculousness.

"He knows Leon beat me, sexually abused me and piled a load of shit on me. He wants me to understand he's not Leon. So he's dedicated to taking it slow," I retorted.

"Sister girl," Daisy whispered.

That was when I felt the change in the room.

And with it, I felt the gentle eyes on me.

I swallowed.

Then I announced, "I'm not sure I'm worthy of him. He's dedicated to proving I am. It's going to take some time. But he wants this, and I definitely want it so we're gonna give it a shot."

"You're scared," Ally noted softly.

"I'm terrified. Two dates, I never had it so good," I replied.

"This makes me happy," Jules put in.

I looked to her. "That's part of the scary. It makes me happy. But most of the scary is it seems I'm making him happy, and he's the kind of man I don't ever want that to stop."

"That's pure Shirleen. More worried about giving than getting," Indy mumbled.

I was struck.

"Say what?" I asked her.

She grinned gently at me. "You put the super-bad into badass, Shirleen. But you're the most selfless person I know." Her grin strengthened, but didn't get less gentle. "Outside all these chickies in this room, of course."

"We're so happy for you, we could spit," Sadie declared, a little grin on her fairy princess face.

"Look at this!" Annette cried, and I looked in the direction of her voice to see she had the massive mirror that sat on the floor opened to expose my enormous and perfectly laid out jewelry display inside.

She was swinging the door open and closed. "You can, like, accessorize then check yourself out to see if it works, like, *right away*."

"Annette," Roxie called impatiently.

Annette turned from the mirror, closing it as she did, and locked eyes on me.

"And woman, if I ever hear you say you're not worthy of anything or anyone, I'm gonna shake you until your teeth rattle. You've got a beautiful soul. Nothing dims that. Not one thing. It might have lived in the shadows for a while, but it surprises nobody that it broke through. So don't you dare talk yourself down, not in front of your girls. Not in front of anyone. Are you understanding me?"

Well, *oowee*.

I'll be damned.

Annette had some badass to her.

"I'm under—" I started.

I didn't get it all out because Jet went flying from the door as it was thrown open.

Everyone turned to it to see Tod, in his flight attendant uniform, tear in.

He slammed the door, looked around and snapped, "I *told you* I was *on my way*! It isn't *easy* getting from DIA into town at rush hour. And you started without me!"

"Chill, sugar. We been waiting *days*, you know we couldn't wait any longer," Daisy said.

"Not even *ten minutes*?" Tod asked.

All the Rock Chicks (save Annette) looked guilty.

Tod turned to me. "Is he cute?"

Tod was Indy and Lee's neighbor. Tod was one half of Tod and Stevie. Tod (and obviously Stevie) was gay.

It wasn't that Tod was gay that he was a Rock Chick. It was arguable seeing as they swung both ways (those ways being both Hot Bunch and Rock Chick), but Tex and Duke, both who worked at Indy's bookstore, both not gay, were also de facto Rock Chicks.

It was just how we rolled.

I didn't know if "hot" translated to "cute" in gay-speak.

Still, I replied, "Mm-hmm."

He leaned back and grinned. "Well, all right."

"Tod can buy you some rubbers," Annette declared.

Tod's eyes got big.

At me.

"You don't have any condoms, honey?" he asked.

"Can we give the condoms a rest?" I requested.

"I'll talk to Eddie," Jet murmured.

I guessed we couldn't.

"Don't talk to Eddie," Indy advised swiftly.

"Why not?" Jet asked.

"Eddie's not a big fan of buying condoms for other dudes," Indy told her.

"Do I want to know this story?" Jet inquired.

"Sure, it's funny," Ally answered, also tossing herself on my bed.

"And it reminds me I might need to stock up on Lip Smackers," Indy muttered.

"Oh for goodness sakes, *I'll* buy you some condoms," Daisy stated. She was now at my jewelry mirror, had it open, and was draping some necklaces around her neck. She turned to me. "Can I borrow these, sugar?"

"I need a drink," Stella announced before I could give approval, or not, to Daisy's request.

"I need three," Tod declared, also throwing himself on my bed. "Who's manning the cocktail shaker?"

"Shirleen, you got some chips?" Ava asked.

Did I have some chips?

I was raising teenage boys.

I had more chips than the Lays factory.

"Yeah, hey," Annette could be heard. She was on her phone. Alarmingly. "I wanna order some pizzas." Yep, Shirleen was alarmed. "You ready? Right. One large veggie. That's for me," she said this last to the room before going back to her phone. "One large pepperoni.

One large sausage. We're gonna need some of that cheesy bread. Two orders. And maybe a salad." She got some looks. "Okay, no salad and three orders of that cheesy bread. Right. You got my account from my number? Right. Cool. Charge it on the card on file. But it's a new address." Her gaze came to me. "What's the address here again?"

Ten voices told her the address.

I'll note, none of those voices was mine.

Annette strolled to the door after giving my address, stating, "Right, thanks. Laterzzzzz." She took the phone from her ear, opened the door and shouted, "Pizza in thirty!"

"Right on!" Sniff shouted back.

Roam had no reply.

"Oh my God! I *need* to borrow these shoes!" Ava wandered out of my walk-in holding my Gucci crystal embellished sandals that I'd bought on a whim because they were fancy and I had nowhere to wear them but they were just so hot I couldn't pass them up. "Luke would *love* these."

Damn.

Now I just had to give them to her.

This was because I held the knowledge that Luke Stark liked his woman in sexy shoes, and just *how* he liked to work things out with those sexy shoes and their heels digging in certain areas of his flesh. And now I couldn't wear those shoes without thinking of those heels digging in Luke Stark's flesh.

Shit.

"Bring those to me," Tod ordered, already twisting his body in a knot to take off his own shoes. "I'm *feeling* those sandals. I'm feeling 'Born This Way.' I'm feeling 'You Make Me Feel Mighty Real.' I'm feeling wig number three, dress number seventeen. No. I'm feeling *shopping*."

Tod, when he was not being a flight attendant, dad to a chow dog called Chowleena, partner to Stevie or the unofficially official Rock Chick wedding planner, was a drag queen called Burgundy Rose.

Ava walked the Guccis over to Tod.

I felt something touch the back of my hand.

I looked to my side.

Jules was there.

"You knew it would happen," she said quietly.

I did.

I sighed.

"They just love you," she continued.

They did.

I sighed again.

Jules smiled.

"I'm on cocktails," Stella announced on her way to the door. "Who wants what?"

"I'll help," Sadie said, following her.

"Cosmo," Roxie ordered.

"Surprise me," Tod put in, bent over the side of my bed, strapping on my Gucci.

"I'm in for a cosmo, but I gotta call Eddie. Tell him he's on his own for dinner," Jet shared.

"He can come over," Annette invited Jet's husband to *my* house. "I'll just call and order more pizza."

"Tell him to go to Lincoln's. Lee's having a team meeting. He can meet the guys there," Indy told Jet.

"Tell him to tell Hank," Roxie added.

"I better call Blanca and let her know she's got Alex for dinner," Jet muttered.

"And I better call Nick and see if he's down with watching Max and Sam for the foreseeable future," Jules said, disengaging from me.

Eddie and Jet, and Jules and Vance had started their broods.

The rest would follow.

And as evidenced with what was right then happening in my bedroom, it wouldn't slow any of them down.

I went to the closet to take off my heels and put on my slippers.

What could I say?

The Rock Chicks were in the house.

And as I've said, I was relatively badass, and the fact remained, I had been ticked at them.

But still.

The truth of it was...

I wouldn't have it any other way.

EIGHT

HOLDING IT TIGHT

Shirleen

"When the time comes, sweetheart, you won't have to worry about condoms. That's the man's domain."

It was later that night.

The Rock Chicks had gone.

The boys were down in their space.

And I'd repoofed my duvet so I could unpoof it my own damned self by lying on it to talk to Moses.

Obviously, I'd told him about the Rock Chick visit.

Yes.

Even the uncomfortable parts about it.

"Great," I murmured.

"Though it would be funny to find out how Lee Nightingale or Kai Mason would react to being asked to buy you condoms," he went on, sounding like he thought it was funny just to think about it.

And hearing that in his voice, it got funny instead of being mortifying.

"Yeah," I replied.

"We're out to your girls."

His tone was entirely different when he said that.

"Yeah," I whispered.

"You talk me up?" he teased.

"I talked me down."

After I said that, I could actually feel his pissed-off vibe coming at me over the phone.

"Don't worry, honey," I assured. "They don't like it any more than you do and didn't mind sharing that."

"I hope so," he stated shortly.

I changed the subject. "Had the talk with the boys about school."

"How'd that go?"

"Told 'em to think on it. I'll give them time to do that and we'll have another chat."

"You get a sense of where they're leaning?"

"Didn't get that shot seeing as the Rock Chicks broke into my house before we could formally end discussions."

I heard him chuckle.

"But that's probably good. They tend to do better when I give them space to sort stuff out on their own," I told him.

"Yeah," he said.

"You have a good night with your girls?" I asked.

"We always do. They're good girls. For them, they're just home. For me, it's like a reunion every time they come home. My daughters, their ages, biweekly reunions instead of them just bein' with me every night."

His tone was again different. And not a good different.

"Darlin'," I whispered.

"It is what it is. But what that is doesn't get better no matter how much time goes by."

"Wish it was different."

There was a silence he didn't fill before he cleared his throat. "Haven't shared that with anyone. Not a friend. Not even my momma."

"Glad you felt safe sharin' it with me."

"Feels good to have you to share it with."

It sure did.

Just like it felt good to have him to text when I was worried about what would happen about Roam at school, then when I was thrilled with what happened about Roam.

I'd never had anything like that with Leon. I'd learned early never to share a fear or a sorrow, and there weren't any triumphs worth sharing. He catalogued any weakness and had a specific skill where he'd time it just right to use them against you when he could make the most damage.

"What're you thinkin'?" Moses asked.

"I was thinkin' that Leon used vulnerabilities against you, so I learned not to share them."

He said nothing to that.

So I spoke.

"I'm sorry, Moses. I get used to this, there'll come a time when I don't compare him to you."

"I wasn't quiet because of that, baby. I was quiet because I was trying to get a rein on bein' pissed he was such a humongous jackass and you had to live for years with that."

That didn't make it any better.

"Maybe we should be a Leon Free Zone," I suggested.

"Why?"

"It messes with me and pisses you off."

"How you gonna work through what he did to you if you don't get it out?"

Good question.

"Might be time to make somethin' else clear about the us I want us to build, Shirleen," he declared. "And that's the fact we gotta be real. We gotta talk. We gotta share. We gotta be there to help the other work shit out and we gotta be open to talk so we can get on working our own shit out."

And here we were.

Again.

"This is where it gets scary because I got more shit to work out than you do," I pointed out.

"If you think I got the job I got lookin' after the kids I see every day and I don't take that home with me and need somewhere to unload it, you're wrong. I been doing that job a long time, and most of the time I can handle it. Sometimes, some kids, it gets under your skin and I need to work it out."

"Who do you work it out with now?" I asked curiously.

"Who do you work Leon out with now?" he returned.

"Mm," I hummed.

"Yeah," he agreed.

And there it was.

Alone was alone in the way we'd both been alone, even having people in our lives.

And it could suck for anyone.

"Never had this," I said softly. "Even with all my girls, who would listen, I didn't wanna bog them down with it. So I never had this."

"Me either," he replied. "Even when I had my wife, I didn't give this to her because she wasn't real interested, and then we had our babies and I didn't bring it home. But it didn't matter. I'd learned by then she wasn't real interested."

One could say I would not have been a big fan of the woman who cheated on Moses Richardson and broke his heart.

But seriously.

She was sounding like a real asshole.

"Got no reply to that?" Moses asked.

"I'm pleading the fifth before I say anything super ugly about the mother of your children."

"You know, you aren't the only one comparing, Shirleen."

Oh boy.

"I don't want to make the same mistakes either," he shared.

I hadn't thought about that.

But it sure made sense.

And I hoped to God Moses never thought of me as a mistake.

"I hear that, honey," I murmured.

"Now, I don't wanna let you go but I'm gonna let you go, because it's getting late and my girls haven't gone to sleep yet. I need to see where they're at. I'll call you tomorrow. And we'll set something up if we can this week. If we can't do that, I want to be on your calendar first chance I got. Next Friday night. Yeah?"

Oh yeah.

"Yes," I agreed.

"Take you out somewhere nice so I can see you in another pretty dress."

I could totally do that.

"I'll look forward to that, Moses."

"Great, baby. You sleep well."

"You too, darlin'."

"'Night, Shirleen."

"Goodnight, Moses."

We hung up and I looked at my feet in their slippers.

I still didn't know how this was happening, me sitting on my bed in my slippers talking to a handsome man about life and our kids and our pasts, and what we wanted in our futures.

I just knew it was happening.

And I was beginning to believe I deserved it.

So I quit looking at my feet in their slippers.

And I started smiling at them.

"You got what on your face?" Moses asked.

"Purple goo."

"Purple goo?"

"A facial. And it's gettin' on my phone. Can I call you back in twenty?"

"It takes twenty minutes to wash purple goo off your face?"

It was the next night.

Moses and I were on the phone again.

He'd texted me that morning to say he'd call that night after talking to the girls.

I'd texted him back to say I'd be looking forward to that call.

He'd then texted me with five options of where we could have dinner Friday night.

I'd texted him to share I liked all five options and it was his choice.

He'd then texted me to ask if it was appropriate for a girl to have three drawers full of makeup and still think she needed more.

I texted him back to give him the news it wasn't only appropriate, it should be encouraged.

He texted to share he wasn't sure he agreed with that.

It was then, me, Shirleen, texted him a tearing-up-laughing emoji.

He'd texted back a smiley-face emoji.

Shit, we were emoji-ing.

Emoji-ing!

Now it was later and he'd called in the middle of a facial.

So I needed to call him back.

"It takes twenty minutes for it to work its magic and then it takes thirty seconds to wash it off," I educated him. "You called right after I brushed it on."

"Just put me on speakerphone."

Oh.

Right.

That'd be the smart way to play it.

I took the phone from my ear and put him on speakerphone.

"You're on speaker," I declared.

Through the speaker, I heard him chuckle.

Boy, a woman could fall in love with that sound.

After he quit doing that, he asked, "Have a good day?"

"You ever tried herding badasses?"

"I spend my days herding kids who think they're badasses, does that count?"

"I'll introduce you to Luke Stark. Then you can tell me your guess at how he reacts to me tellin' him to sit his ass down and write out his time sheets."

Another chuckle.

Yes, a woman could fall in love with that sound.

Okay.

Would it sound too eager for me to bring it up?

Damn.

I was just going to bring it up.

He wanted us open. Real.

I still tried for casual.

"So did you talk to your girls?"

"Yeah. Though Judith has a study date, *here*, with her boyfriend Wednesday night, other than that, it's father-daughter time."

I was happy for him he had that.

But I found it disappointing.

"We can have phone dates," he said.

"I'll take it," I whispered.

"I'm glad, baby," he whispered back.

"And just to say, I hear you, my man, about this boy Judith is dating. Roam dates white girls. He dates some sisters, but mostly he dates white girls. Sniff, however, sees black girls. Almost exclusive. There's a white girl here and there, but I'm sensing the sister is just his type. But I got an issue with Roam when he's with a white girl, and I don't got an issue with Sniff, because he sees the beauty of a sister. And I know that's messed up. It's just the way I feel."

"Yeah. And I just want her to be happy. This kid, his name is Jaxon, with an X, by the way."

"Oh boy," I muttered.

"Yeah," he said. "It's not there. To him Judith is a pretty girl. She's his girlfriend. He's not weird with me. They're just people."

"World fucks that up when you get older," I noted.

"Right. And I don't wanna be the one who fucks that up. I don't want to be the one who points it out that he's dating a black girl and he needs to get her culture, her people, and respect it when that isn't on his radar."

"It's gotta be *partially* on his radar, Moses, unless he's blind."

"I'm not sure it is. He's just really into her."

I couldn't even stop myself from uttering, "Gulk."

He totally got me and that was not about the kid being white.

"I know. When'd she stop being seven?" he asked.

"Ten years ago," I pointed out.

"Yeah," he muttered, then went on, "In the end, it doesn't matter. Unless he's hurting her or changing her personality in ways that concern me, I just gotta let it play out."

"Yeah, you just do."

"You ever talk to the boys about them treating girls now with a mind to how they'd feel having their own girls in the future?"

"Not yet. But I'll be leveling that Shirleen Lecture on them in between waiting on them getting their Follow Up Shirleen Lecture about going to college."

That got me another chuckle before he said, "Ever think there'd be a time you'd be scheduling lectures to your teenage boys?"

"Dreamed it every day, but no. Never."

There was a beat of silence then he asked, "You wanted kids?"

"Wanted a boy. Least one. One I could make into a good man. One who'd take care of his momma."

"And then God gave you two," he remarked.

"And then God gave me two," I repeated. "We shouldn't bitch, Moses. We're so lucky. We both got good kids."

"We are, baby," he agreed. "Don't I know that. Damned lucky."

It was heavy and it went on with the heavy as Moses shared about some of the kids at Gilliam and the obstacles they faced in their lives to get them on the right path.

I took us out of the heavy when I felt he was ready by sharing about the antics of the Rock Chicks (the tamer ones, we were starting out, I didn't want to scare him) just to try to make him laugh.

We talked and we talked, and we talked some more.

We even talked through me washing my face.

And a whole lot longer.

In fact, I was in bed, my hair twisted up, my silk scarf wrapped around it, under the covers in the dark after we'd talked out his kids, the Rock Chicks, movies we liked, books we'd read, places we'd been, dream vacations we wanted to take, and Moses's sweet honey voice was in my ear, soothing me like a lullaby.

He didn't miss it.

"Gonna let you go, sweetheart."

"I don't want you to let me go," I mumbled.

And I really, *really* didn't.

"And I don't wanna let you go, but you sound about ready to pass out."

I was.

"Okay, you can let me go."

"Call you tomorrow."

"Okay."

"Thanks for listening, baby," he said.

"Thanks for talking, and also thanks for listening," I replied.

He chuckled.

And hearing it, that was where I wanted to end it.

"'Night, Moses."

"'Night, baby."

I pressed my phone to my chest after we disconnected and I did not *even* care I slept with it there.

Holding him close.

Holding his goodness to me.

His promise.

Holding it tight.

"Say what?" I asked during our phone date Thursday night (we'd had one Wednesday night too, bee T dub).

"I'm reading the *Rock Chicks*. I'm at the beginning. Indy and Lee."

Damn.

I didn't know how I was feeling about this.

"When do you come in?" he queried.

"Uh, the next one. Jet and Eddie."

"Do you know this Kristen Ashley person who wrote them?"

"It's a penname. It's really someone who used to work at Indy's bookstore."

"Did she fire them?"

"No. But the books took off so she writes full time now."

"Goes on book tours?"

"Apparently, unless you sell a bucketload, that doesn't happen. That is, unless it's your own dime."

He sounded confused. "But she has a schedule of appearances on her website."

Hmm.

He'd checked the website.

"That's just some woman in Phoenix Jane hired to pretend she's Kristen Ashley. Jane's not super social. She'd lose it if she had to go to a book signing."

"Ah," he mumbled. Then he asked, "You okay I'm reading these?"

Yikes, but he could read me already.

Even over the phone.

"Well, uh, they met me when, uh…"

"Babe," he clipped.

I shut up and not only at his tone.

He'd called me "babe," not "baby" not "sweetheart."

That was totally Hot Bunch.

Toe-tah-lee.

I'd heard Luke Stark call an eighty-three-year-old woman, who'd come into the office to hire the guys because she was concerned her children were slowly poisoning her, "babe."

She'd blushed like a schoolgirl.

And Moses was getting impatient with me being an idiot.

He was into me.

He called me every night.

We were going out to a nice dinner the first night he was free after his girls went back to their mom's.

I needed to get over it.

"Actually, I'm pretty funny in those books," I told him. "It's just that, in the early ones, I was drug-dealing, poker-game-running funny."

"This isn't going to surprise me, Shirleen," he reminded me.

"Right," I muttered. "Uh," I went on, "have you thought, you know, if this works with us—"

Moses cut me off. "*If* it does?"

"Well, yeah."

"You don't think it's working?"

"It is now."

"You think it's going to quit working?"

"I hope not."

"So how 'bout we use the word 'when' this works."

This was not a suggestion.

"It doesn't fit in my question," I explained.

"What's your question?"

"Okay, *when* this works and I meet your girls, and then I got a question after that. Do you think that fits?"

"It could be *when* we're confident this is working and you meet my girls."

It was safe to say Shirleen was getting irritated.

"My man, are you honestly tellin' me what to say?"

"I'm telling you not to say or think negatively that it might not work."

"I can tell *you* right about *now* I'm thinkin' negative thoughts about a man telling me which word to use."

I knew what he thought about that.

He thought that was funny, and I knew he did because I heard him laughing.

"You think I'm being funny?" I asked.

"No. I think it's all kinds of good you got no problem tellin' me like it is when I'm being a jackass."

"Well...*humph*."

Yep.

I humphed.

But the situation warranted it.

"So, what was the question you wanted to ask about *when* we know this is working and you meet my girls," he prompted.

"I know *this* girl's nerves are getting worked by her man."

"Yeah," he whispered, that honey pouring right in my ear. "Like that. 'Her man.'"

I shut up.

But I liked it too.

Legs-getting-restless-while-I-was-lying-on-my-bed liked it.

"Baby, you were gonna ask me a question?" he pushed.

"What are you gonna tell them about the woman their daddy's datin' being an ex-poker-game-running drug-dealer."

After I asked that, I held my breath.

I didn't have to hold it long because Moses answered immediately.

"*When* the time is right, which will be when they're older, I'm gonna tell them you used to run games and deal drugs."

"Say what?" I whispered.

"By then they'll know you, Shirleen. They'll know you're good for me. They'll know Roam and Sniff and what you did for them. They'll have met your friends and know how much they love you. And I don't keep anything from my girls, not anything that big. It's disrespect. So they're too young now. But when they can get it, they'll know."

I didn't know what to think about that either.

"I know my girls, baby," he went on. "And when you do, you'll get that's the right way to play it."

"That scares me."

"I bet," he said gently. "Sadly, that's the penance you have to keep paying after you do shit in your life that affected other lives in bad ways that you regret."

"Yeah," I muttered.

"It'll be okay," he assured.

I hoped so.

"It'll be okay, Shirleen," he repeated.

"I hope so," I replied.

"Baby, listen to me," he urged.

I was listening but I listened harder.

"Do you think I'd be with you if I didn't think they'd see in you what I see in you?" he asked.

That made sense.

"No," I whispered.

"I wouldn't do them like that and I wouldn't do *you* like that," he continued.

"Okay, Moses."

"So don't worry about it."

That might not be possible.

"Okay, Moses," I lied.

"My beautiful woman is totally lying," he muttered.

"*Humph*."

Yep.

Even though he called me his beautiful woman, I humphed again.

He chuckled again.

Then he got serious. "We had our bad, Shirleen. It's time for our good. I'm committed to giving you that. Now what I need from you is for you to believe in it. But don't worry. I'm okay with taking that slow too. Just as long as we're moving forward."

"You're annoying when you've *been* annoying and then you're all sweet."

"Wish right now I could be a different kind of sweet," he murmured.

I shivered.

"Please tell me your boys have plans tomorrow night so I can make out in the car with you for at least an hour after I take you out to dinner," he stated.

Another shiver.

"They got plans," I promised.

"Good," he said low.

And...

Another shiver.

It was time to change the subject.

"I will state, in my defense, as you read those books, that I told Ava it was a bad idea to go to Vito's house prior to her nearly flipping her SUV over onto I-25 with me in it."

"I'm sorry?" he asked quietly.

Perhaps I picked the wrong subject.

"Uh, spoiler alert," I mumbled.

"You were in an SUV that nearly flipped onto I-25?"

"It didn't."

"You were in an SUV that nearly flipped onto I-25?"

"We were being chased. By an, um, mobster."

Moses fell silent.

"You might want to get into the frame of mind of me and all my friends as fictional characters before you get any deeper in those books," I advised.

"Lee told me his wife was kidnapped three times."

"Um..."

"Were *you* ever kidnapped?"

"No," I said swiftly.

"Did anything of yours explode?" he asked.

"Uh, no."

"Why was there an 'uh' before that 'no?'"

"Just that, you know, I don't want you to get overly concerned when you read about the fact I shot someone in my living room when they broke into my house 'cause a bad guy didn't want Mace, Lee, Eddie, Hank and the boys to keep doing what Mace, Lee, Eddie, Hank and the boys were doing. Primarily, trying to get him incarcerated."

"Why didn't you call nine one one?"

"There wasn't time. Seein' as I had my boys with me, I had to look out for them and he shot first."

More silence.

Scary silence.

"It's all good now," I said quickly.

"Are there any more of them left?" he asked.

"More of what?"

"Rock Chicks."

"Only me."

"You're not getting kidnapped and shot at on my watch."

I grinned. "Good to know."

"Jesus," he muttered.

"Maybe you shouldn't read those books," I suggested.

"Are you in danger working for Lee Nightingale now?" he asked.

Hmm.

"Shirleen," he growled when I didn't respond immediately.

"Define your concept of danger."

That got another growl, just one that didn't come with words associated with it.

It was hot.

Before my legs got restless again, I told him, "Lee and the boys try to keep the action out of the office."

"*Try?*"

"Sometimes they fail," I admitted.

"Fucking hell," he whispered.

"It isn't their fault," I defended. "Obviously they don't *want* bad guys to storm through the front door and shoot up the joint."

"Holy fuck," he bit off.

"But that hasn't happened for a while," I shared.

"*When* this works, we might need to have a conversation about your employment."

"Baby," I said softly, "I love my job. I love those boys. We have protocols should anything like that happen, one such protocol being put in place when that Balducci brother invaded. I was under lock and key with the police en route, a skilled, armed man between the bad guys and me, and Lee and Luke sprinting up the steps. We have tight security. No one even gets in that building without us knowing, and if they were a threat, I'd be protected. Swear."

He didn't share he was appeased by this explanation.

"Each one of those men would take a bullet for me, make no mistake about that, Moses."

"That, I know," he replied.

I drew in breath and let it out, saying, "And I'm pretty good at taking care of myself."

"Mm," he murmured.

"But can I tell you how sweet it is you're worried?" I asked.

"You can tell me that," he said.

I grinned.

"I'm glad I didn't have to live through all that shit with you," he noted. "I foresee a kidnapping if I did, that being me kidnapping you."

That got him another grin as I said, "Talk to any Hot Bunch member. They'll share just how much unfun they were having when it was happening."

"Hot Bunch?"

He hadn't gotten to that part in the books yet, obviously.

"The men."

"And the women are the Rock Chicks."

"Yeah."

"And the Rock Chicks?"

I didn't know what he was asking.

"What about them?"

"Did they think it was unfun?"

Hmm again.

"They didn't think *all* of it was fun," I hedged.

"Say, the explosions," he started to break it down.

"That there's a good example, because we all thought it was pretty funny Tex exploded that warehouse where he'd been taken after he was kidnapped. But we didn't think it was funny at all when Stella's apartment got blown up."

"Maybe we should quit talking about this."

"I hear that," I said quietly. "And maybe you should give those books a miss."

"I am absolutely reading those books."

"Moses—"

"I need to know what I'm getting into."

"Maybe that's a good call," I mumbled. "But, remember, it's been years and I've got no ill effects after I got conked on the head when Slick and his boys shot up my poker game."

"Jesus Christ," he whispered.

I couldn't help it.

I grinned again.

"You're totally gonna love the Rock Chicks," I told him.

"I thought I would. Not sure now if that's true."

"They love me straight to their souls."

"Then you're right, sweetheart. I'll love them."

And that made me grin again.

We talked a lot longer.

And I grinned a lot more.

We ended our conversation with me lulled half asleep with Moses's sweet voice sounding in my ear.

I fell totally asleep yet again with my phone held to my chest.

But this time it was different.

This time, everything was different.

Because tomorrow, for the first time in a long time, I had something amazing and beautiful and exciting to look forward to.

Tomorrow, I was going to see Moses again.

NINE

REBORN

Shirleen

The next night, I opened the door to my house.

I stood there in my dress and heels, hair done, makeup refreshed, staring at the handsome man on my doorstep wearing a *café au lait* button up, a chocolate-brown blazer, his eyes warming, his lips forming a sexy smile upon seeing me...

And I was reborn.

His warm, rich voice came at me, covering my skin, washing the last of the dust away at the same time it seeped in, through the skin, the flesh, the bone, to fill my marrow with liquid goodness.

"Ready to go?"

I stood there, unable to move.

"Or you wanna show me your place?" he asked.

He was so beautiful.

So beautiful.

And I had it in my power to make him mine.

Like I had it in my power to keep on keeping on the way I'd been keeping on and told Daisy I was not going to help Jet find her daddy.

But I made my choice.

Then I helped Jet find her daddy.

Like I had it in my power to stay detached, stay removed, not get involved.

But I made my choice.

And I became friends with Jet. I renewed my friendship with Daisy. And with time, the rest of them came along.

Like I had it in my power when things were heating up on the streets with Jules being a vigilante and I had a choice to make.

And I made that choice.

Then Darius and me got out of the game.

Like I had it in my power when the worst that could happen happened, and Roam and Jules both got shot, Jules nearly got dead, this happening while they were looking out for each other, and I wanted Jules's kids under my roof so I could look after them.

And I made that choice.

Then I made it happen.

I'd been experiencing the longest, slowest rebirth maybe of all time.

A rebirth I had to fight for.

And could have died for.

But I kept at it.

And I would never be at peace. Not after all I'd done.

But I was going to take this new life I'd chosen.

And I was going to live it up.

"Baby, you okay?" Moses asked.

Only then did I move.

I reached out a hand, grasped him by his button down, and pulled him into my house.

Into me.

His hands immediately came to my waist.

And with my head tipped back, his lips came immediately to my mouth.

I clamped a hand on the side of his head.

And that was when Moses kissed me.

I moved backwards, taking him with me.

His lips detached.

Oh no.

"Shirleen."

"Close the door."

"Baby."

"The boys are gone."

"Sweetheart."

I let his shirt go so I could clamp both of my hands on his head.

"Please," I whispered.

Moses looked into my eyes.

He then turned to shut the door.

I heard the lock go.

Then he turned back to me.

And I again had his mouth.

I took it. Lord, did I. I took from it and let him take from me. I pressed tight to his strong length, walking backwards, leading him with me, drinking from that sweet mouth, drinking *deep*.

When I sensed my bedroom door, I shifted us, his head came up again and he stopped us.

"You sure?" he whispered.

"I have only been more sure of one thing in my life. Offering my boys a home," I answered.

His warm brown eyes got warmer.

Then they got hot.

And suddenly I wasn't leading Moses Richardson anywhere.

He was taking me where he wanted us to be.

Which, shortly thereafter, was us falling on my bed, him on top.

That was a way I did not mind in the slightest my duvet getting unpoofed.

He was hot and heavy with his mouth, his tongue, but he went gentle and slow with his hands.

Until I pulled his hand up to my breast, curled it around, arched into it, and when he slid his thumb over my nipple, I moaned into his mouth.

This was it.

This was the good stuff.

Real.

Open.

Safe.

I believed.

I believed in that.

And I believed I deserved to have it.

I pulled at his jacket.

He yanked it off and tossed it away.

I tugged his shirt out of his pants, dove my hands under and felt his smooth, warm skin.

Lord.

Heaven.

"You feel good," I whispered against his mouth when he stopped kissing me so he could nibble my lower lip.

His thumb slid back over my nipple, and I whimpered a little and arched into him again.

"You feel better," he rumbled, slanted his head and kissed me again.

And again.

Then more.

He made me dizzy with it.

Lost to it.

Until it hit me I wanted even more.

I went after the buttons of his shirt.

His mouth went after my neck as I undid the buttons of his shirt.

That felt *nice.*

"Please tell me you brought condoms," I breathed in his ear.

Another button open.

"I put three of 'em in my wallet the night after the Rock Chicks broke in."

Oowee.

I smiled.

And opened another button.

He lifted his head to catch my smile.

Then he dropped it to kiss me again.

I forgot about his buttons because his kiss was so sweet, so hot, I had to hold on or I'd get an ice-cream headache at the same time I melted into my bed.

And I had to get serious about that, and in doing so might have curled my nails into the flesh at his back.

He instantly let my mouth go to lift up a smidge in order to undo his cuffs then he yanked the still half-buttoned shirt over his head.

I caught sight of his wide pecs, the swells and planes that made his midriff, his flat stomach, the crease of his navel.

And it was then, I lost control.

In other words, I attacked.

He was on his back and I'd yanked my skirt up to straddle him, but hunched over to get my mouth on that chest.

His skin felt good.

It tasted better.

"Baby," he murmured.

I licked his nipple.

His hand clamped on the back of my neck. "Fuck, *baby*."

He was all kinds of goodness to offer to go slow.

But enough of that shit.

I had nails to his abs, mouth to his neck, when I felt his fingers tug the skirt of my red, long-blouson-sleeved, cold shoulder dress.

"Want this off," he murmured.

I lifted up and twisted my arms behind me to get at the zip.

He curled up to sitting and said, "Before you dislocate a shoulder, let me."

He was smiling at me.

I went in and kissed that smile off his lips.

The zip went down fast.

The dress then went up, up…

I broke my mouth from his and lifted my arms…

And away.

His eyes fell to my body.

I clasped his bristly cheeks to lift his head so I could kiss him again, but I got nowhere.

Except on my back with Moses on top of me.

"I liked the dress," he growled.

"Good," I pushed out, staring into his face, that face wearing an expression I'd never seen before.

I saw it with my eyes, but I felt it with my lady parts.

Nice.

"But the underwear…" he went on.

I had to admit, I had a thing for underwear.

Lacy underwear.

"Did you know we'd be right here, right now?" he asked, his hand smoothing over my side, starting to go in.

"Um…no. If you're asking if I wore these for you, it's not even my best set."

His expression shifted to another one I'd never seen before and my lady parts rippled.

Hot.

"Stop talking," he ordered, his hand now at my belly.

"Okay," I whispered.

His eyes held mine as his hand went down.

"Good?" he said softly.

I nodded.

His fingertips hit an edge of lace.

"Good?" he repeated gently.

"Yes, baby," I answered.

His fingertips slid in, more, down, curved, the middle one gliding tight.

My lips parted, I hooked my ankle around his calf and my nails *definitely* dug into his flesh.

"I'll take that as good," he rumbled appreciatively.

"Yeah," I panted.

He kissed me.

He stroked me.

He built it in me.

And I sucked his tongue deep when he made me explode.

He was cupping my sex and nuzzling my ear when I came down holding him to me.

"How late you wanna be for our reservation?" he murmured into my ear.

I'd had mine.

He'd given that to me.

He hadn't had his and the evidence of that was pressed against my thigh.

"Mm? Sweetheart?" he prompted against the skin at the side of my neck.

He was hard.

And if I said I was hungry or if that was as far as I could go right then, he would have put his shirt on, his kickass blazer, helped me zip up my dress.

And we'd go.

"Moses," I called.

He lifted his head and looked down at me.

Boy, this man was *beautiful*.

"I don't care if I ever eat again," I declared.

Maybe that was dramatic.

But a point needed to be made.

I made it.

A flash of white shown behind his lips as a flash of heat shot through his eyes and he dipped his head and kissed me again.

We went slower. He took his time. In some far part of my mind that wasn't all about Moses, what he looked like, felt like, smelled like, sounded like, how he was making me feel, all of it so magnificent it was hard to fathom, and gorgeous to revel in, I'd realize that first orgasm was for me, but it was also so we could dial it back and if we carried on, he could give me this.

This intimacy.

These moments.

Being right there, firm in our nows, and doing that in order to make the most of it, but also make this the best memory it could be.

And he made it the best through his touch, his murmured words, his taking my bra and panties off me like he was unwrapping a package that he knew what was inside, and he wanted it so badly he wished to draw out the experience.

And he showed me him and how his strength and beauty were in every inch (and of a few particular inches, there were a *lot* of them).

And when he slid inside me, he'd given me enough kisses.

He'd given me enough touches.

He'd tasted enough with his tongue.

He'd let me taste enough with mine.

So we were right there, firm in our nows, staring into each other's eyes, wrapped around each other's bodies, as he inched inside me slowly and I knew I'd never forget a second of it.

When he'd filled me, when I saw the lazy hit his lids and the possession curl his lips, I stroked his cheeks with both my hands, lifted my head so we were so close there was nothing between our eyes but lashes and whispered, "I love my now."

Only then did Moses kiss me again as he started moving inside me, making love to me, making my now even better.

And sealing the deal on Shirleen reborn.

"You WANT me to call the restaurant and see if they still got our table open, or any table open, or you wanna give it up and just go to Arby's?"

Had to admit, I loved that his go-to was Arby's.

Moses and I were lying across my bed. The fluffy folds of my dove-gray duvet (with just a hint of lavender) were totally demolished seeing as not only had we had sex on them, Moses had pulled them out from under us to have them kinda covering our bottom halves.

And I was resting down his side, but chest to chest with him, smoothing my finger over the creases at the bridge of his nose.

Up that close, they were *fascinating*.

"Shirleen," he called quietly.

I looked into his eyes. "You hungry, honey?"

"I want to leave this bed like I want someone to drill a hole in my head. But your boys—"

"They won't be home for hours."

He grinned, rolled me, then he was chest to my chest, sweeping the tip of his thumb against the bottom edge of my lip.

"Right then, I'm good right here with you for hours, sweetheart," he murmured, watching his thumb move.

I loved that.

Still.

"I should feed you something," I offered.

I wanted to make him my Coca-Cola ham with my famous mashed potatoes and my momma's flakey biscuits.

I wanted Roam to grill him burgers.

I wanted Sniff to knock his socks off with something he stole from Bobby Flay.

I wanted everything and I wanted it right then. I wanted it all to happen within the next few seconds. For the first time since I could remember, I could *not wait* for what was next up in my life.

But even so, I never wanted to move from that bed.

His other hand shoved in at the small of my back and started up my spine.

"I neglected to mention it at the time, seeing as I was occupied, but I like your room, baby. You got style."

I grinned up at him.

His hand at my spine became a steel arm around my back, and

his thumb at my lip became a hand clamped on my neck when a pounding came at the door.

"Who's in there?" Roam shouted.

"Uh-oh," I whispered.

Another pound came at the door.

"Shirleen! You okay?" Sniff shouted.

"Fuck," Moses whispered.

"You got five seconds to open this door!" Roam yelled.

"We're armed!" Sniff declared.

"*Fuck*," Moses whispered, gently but swiftly rolling us both up.

"*One!*" Roam barked.

I hit my feet and had my panties in my hand as given to me by Moses half a second later.

"*Two!*" Sniff roared.

I was shoving my feet in the holes when I yelled, "It's me! I'm fine!"

There was silence while I pulled my panties up.

Moses handed me my bra.

"Whose truck is in the driveway?" Roam shouted.

"Just give us a second," I called.

"*Us?*" Sniff thundered.

"Shit," Moses muttered.

"A second!" I snapped.

I put on my bra double time and saw Moses had his pants and unbuttoned shirt on when he handed me my dress.

I pulled that over my head while he put his socks and shoes on.

He zipped me up.

I left my shoes where Moses had tossed them and stomped to the door.

"Shirleen," Moses called urgently.

I didn't listen.

I marched right to the door.

I did this thinking the boys would retreat to the living room.

And it would be there I could ream them.

And *good*.

I hauled the door open and saw the boys standing right there.

Their eyes hit me then they shot beyond me.

To Moses.

"You!" Roam shouted.

"Motherfucker!" Sniff shouted.

They both pushed in.

"Boys!" I yelled, reaching out and grabbing Sniff's arm.

He shrugged me off as they faced off with Moses.

I had their backs but I still could see they took in the bed.

The air in the room became stifling.

"You did our mom right under our roof?" Roam bellowed.

I froze.

Solid.

Suspended in time.

And as I hovered there, a vision filled my mind.

Words on paper.

Perspectives of American Military Action in Vietnam

By Roam Jackson

Roam Jackson.

Roam *Jackson*.

"Right now, you both need to cool down," Moses's voice tumbled through the room, taking me out of my stupor.

"Your mom?"

That came from my mouth and it sounded hoarse.

Forced from me.

Tortured.

Roam jerked around towards me, angry.

Sniff turned towards me, also angry.

They both caught one look at me and stilled.

Completely.

Suddenly, it looked like Roam was preparing to take a step away, but he stopped himself.

Though he started talking.

Fast.

"Not our mom. Sorry. I'm sorry. You're not our mom. You're you. Like, independent and you got it together and you dress real nice and you got a great crib and you can boss around the guys and they don't care because you're badass like that and you're like, your own woman. With like, your own life. And you're just, like, not anyone's. You're yours. You're not anyone's mom. You're Shirleen."

"Shut your mouth, boy," I whispered.

He shut his mouth but he looked sick.

My Roam who didn't expose anything, he looked *sick*.

Not sick.

Wounded.

My eyes shifted to Sniff.

His torso was rocking slightly, his gaze not meeting mine, but he'd moved, standing partially in front of Roam like he was preparing to be his shield.

I walked their way, slow, on bare feet.

When I got to them, I lifted a hand to Sniff.

He flinched when I touched his cheek, but I didn't bother myself with that.

I slid my fingers back into his thick hair, curling them around his skull.

Then I reached long and high, to Roam.

I did the same with him, the pads of my fingers gliding over his short-cropped hair, curving in.

And when I got my hands on what was mine, I gathered it to me, *hard*, yanking them in, until all of our foreheads collided.

"Shirleen," Sniff whispered, his hand had come to my hip, maybe to steady himself, but it stayed there, gripping tight.

I dug their heads into mine.

"You're *my boys. Mine.*"

That wasn't hoarse.

It was guttural.

It sounded like it came from an animal.

And maybe I was an animal in that moment.

A lioness.

"Shirleen," Roam whispered, his hand coming to my hip, sliding back, pressing in.

My eyeballs shifted to him.

"Don't you ever say I'm not your momma, boy, you hear me?" I demanded.

"Yeah. Yeah, Shirleen, yeah." His words were fast, conciliatory.

Greedy.

My eyeballs shifted to Sniff.

"You ever gonna say anything like that, Sniff?"

"No, Shirleen, never. Not ever."

"You sign your assignments Sniff Jackson?" I asked.

"Well...yeah," he answered, like it was the stupidest question he'd ever heard.

And that was all I could stand.

So that was when I went down.

"Boys!" Moses called sharply.

But my boys had their hands on me.

They *had me*.

They caught me before I fell. And like every time, Sniff gave into his big brother and he let Roam lift me into his arms and hold me close as he walked me out of my bedroom, down the hall of our home, to our living room where he put me on the couch next to him and gathered me in his arms.

And I wept.

I sobbed.

I held on to my boy.

Until I realized something crucial was missing.

I pulled my face out of his neck and saw Sniff standing close to us, hovering.

"You better get down here before she blows," Roam warned. "Again," he finished.

Sniff moved, burrowing in.

I was still a mess, and only slightly recovering from my episode, but they were teenagers and they hadn't yet learned to read a woman right, so I was in no shape at all for Roam to announce, "I wanna make it official. I wanna go to a court and get the name Roman Jackson. I'm eighteen now and I can do that. I don't want anyone asking me what Roam means anymore, and I don't want anyone wondering why my name isn't the same as yours."

The holler that tore from me probably shook the windows.

"Shit," Roam muttered over my head.

"Too soon," Sniff muttered over my head too.

Roam decided to pack it all in since the damage was done.

"You know, while you're in this state, Sniff wants his name changed to Julien Jackson, for you…and Jules."

My body started bucking with my tears, but fortunately this time it was silent.

"No offense to you, Shirleen, but you kinda can't make Shirleen into a dude's name," Sniff said.

The sound of my choked laughter could be heard through my continued tears.

If it happened for them, it didn't matter that it had happened for me.

But like it was for me, it was going to happen for them.

It was going to happen for my sons.

They were going to let the old go.

And be reborn.

"Shit, is she ever gonna quit crying?" Sniff asked Roam.

That was when I pushed myself up and found I was sitting between them on the couch, both of them turned to me, their arms around me, caging me in.

I grabbed hold of Sniff's jaw, gave it a gentle squeeze and let it go, saying, "Son, if you curse in front of me one more time—"

"Roam cursed and you didn't give him sh…stuff for it," Sniff clipped.

I turned to Roam and grabbed his jaw, gave it a gentle squeeze, and let it go, saying, "You need to mind that mouth, son."

"Shirleen, you got a worse mouth than either of us do," Roam pointed out.

"I'm an adult."

"We're both eighteen," Sniff reminded me.

"There's worse we could do," Roam added.

This was all true.

Stymied.

"When I'm not feeding you or putting a roof over your heads, you can talk however you like," I decreed.

Roam shook his head, his lips twitching.

Sniff rolled his eyes, his lips twitching.

They totally were not going to quit cursing.

Lord.

My boys.

My boys.

Mine.

Roam's lip twitch vanished as something caught his attention, his face went hard, and he instantly announced, "What I'd like to talk about now is what this player is doin' here."

Oh boy.

I faced front to see Moses standing, looking hot, arms crossed on his chest, still no blazer (though he'd buttoned his shirt), smiling indulgently down at me.

I knew my mascara was everywhere.

Damn.

"Get me a tissue, Sniff," I ordered.

He did not get me a tissue.

He pushed up to his feet. "Give us an explanation, Shirleen."

Oh boy.

I pushed up to my feet and Roam came up with me.

"You do not give the orders in this house," I said to Sniff.

"You didn't know we'd come back," Roam accused me.

"What are you doing back?" I rapped out, though I had to admit I was curious.

"You asked us seven thousand times if we'd be gone on Friday and how long we'd be out, and you were in your room every night gabbin' on the phone, and you had a full Rock Chick Gathering in your friggin' bedroom, so it was hard to miss you were planning a little somethin' somethin'," Roam explained.

"And anyway, you didn't even *try* to hide those roses," Sniff put in.

Hell.

"Not real good with the covert, are you, baby?" Moses teased.

I shot him big eyes.

He shot me a big smile.

"We'll talk to *you* in a minute," Roam bit off.

"Roam!" I snapped.

He shot me a scowl.

I turned to Sniff. "So you knew I had something planned with a gentleman friend and you came home and pounded on my bedroom door?"

"We gotta look out for you," Roam answered for Sniff.

"Yeah, that's like, *our job*," Sniff added.

Okay.

Now I couldn't be pissed at them.

Shit.

"And we looked out for you and found out you got yourself tangled up with some player," Roam finished.

"He's not a player, Roam," I said quietly.

"Yeah, he's not, why's he all cool with you makin' sure we're gone before he'll come get you for a date? Hunh? Why won't he walk up and knock on the door like a man and meet your sons like..." Roam leaned into me, "*a man?*"

All good questions.

"Moses has daughters and we were going to give it some time and *when*," I slid my eyes to Moses before I looked back at Roam, "we were confident in what was building between us, we were going to bring all of you into it."

Roam shut his mouth.

Apparently that was a good answer.

Thank the Lord.

"You got daughters?" Sniff asked Moses.

Shit.

Roam reached behind me and smacked Sniff up the backside of his head.

"Dude," he warned low.

"What?" Sniff asked. "That's cool. Shirleen's got two boys. This works with this guy, she might get some girls. That's pretty awesome."

Lord *God*, I loved that kid.

"How about we try this again," Moses decided to officially enter the conversation. He walked forward with his hand up. "I'm Moses Richardson and I really, *really* like your momma."

He aimed his hand at Roam first.

Roam looked at it a beat before he took it and shook it.

When they let go, he offered it to Sniff.

Sniff took it and shook it and they let go.

Moses then took my hand and led me one step toward him.

Both boys closed in at my back.

Yep.

Loved those kids.

"Now, sweetheart, I'm gonna go and let you be with your boys tonight," he said, giving my hand a squeeze.

"Moses—" I started.

"You don't have to do that," Sniff said quickly.

"Yeah, we...maybe, uh...didn't play this right," Roam put in.

"And Shirleen's got a pretty dress on," Sniff continued.

"So, yeah, maybe we should just head back out and..." Roam let that trail.

Moses kept hold of my hand but looked between the boys.

"I think tonight was a big night for all of you." He looked down at me. "Rain check? Tomorrow night?"

"No really, you guys should go out," Sniff said, again quickly.

But it was a different kind of quickly.

I turned suspicious eyes to Sniff. "What's going on?"

He shook his head. "Nothin'. We just...Roam and me just wanted to talk to you tomorrow night."

"About what?" I asked.

"Tomorrow night," Roam put in firmly. "Go out with, uh...Mr. Richardson here and we'll get into it then."

My heart squeezed.

But my eyes hit the ceiling.

"Oh Lord," I looked between them, "which of you got who pregnant?"

"Shirleen!" Sniff bit off.

"Neither, Shirleen, Jesus," Roam huffed out.

"Then what do you need to talk to me about tomorrow night?" I asked.

"Baby, think maybe now is the time I should—" Moses started, giving my hand another squeeze.

"I'm goin' to work for Lee after I graduate," Roam cut him off to declare.

Okay.

All right.

When they were interns, this was fine. They worked computer stuff and watched monitors in the (relative) safety of the office. I could handle the idea of them becoming members of the team when it was all future. All fantasy.

But then it wasn't *real*. It wasn't Roam having his own bulletproof vest in the *locker room*.

I felt the vapors coming on.

"And I'm going into the Army," Sniff announced.

Say...

What?

The *Army*?
The United States Army that fought *wars*?
It was official.
I had the vapors.
For certain.

TEN

FUTURE WAS BRIGHT

Shirleen

"Babe."

That was Moses.

"Nope," I snapped, listening to my phone ring in my ear as I paced my living room.

"Shirleen."

That was Sniff.

"Unh-unh," I bit out, still listening.

"C'mon, Shirleen."

That was Roam.

I didn't have to reply to him.

Lee picked up.

"Hey, Shirleen. Everything good?"

"So you had some conversations with my boys about their futures, hunh?"

"Oh shit," Lee muttered.

"Hell yeah, oh shit. You think to talk to me about that?" I asked heatedly.

When he spoke again, he sounded mildly confused. "They're already recruits. I thought you were on board with that."

My voice was pitched so high, it was a wonder all my crystal didn't shatter when I demanded, "*You told Sniff to go into the Army!*"

"Shirleen—"

"The enemy *shoots at you* when you're in the Army, Lee," I educated him.

"I know, Shirleen, I was in the Army, remember?" Lee returned.

I ignored that.

"Or they blow you up with land mines and shit."

"Have you talked with Sniff about this?" Lee asked.

"Yeah, he said, 'I'm going into the Army.' Then, after I fought off an attack of the vapors, he shared, 'Lee and the guys think it's a good idea.' So that was when I got my phone and called to *lay you out*."

"He wants something that's his," Lee said low.

And that low caught my attention.

Lee kept at me.

"He's been in Roam's shadow for years. He needs out from that. He needs to find out who he is without his brother always at his side. The right groundwork has been laid for him to be the man he wants to be, but he's gotta walk that path alone now so in the end, who he becomes...it's his."

Goddamn, I hated it when these men made sense.

"And Roam?" I clipped out. "He's eighteen, Lee, and you're gonna take him on?"

"He knows he has six months in the office working with Brody. Working with Jack. Working with Monty so he can learn how intel that's gathered is formed into tactics and strategy. Working with *you* to understand the business side of things."

"And that puts him at just over eighteen and a half and then you think he's all good?" I asked.

"No," Lee retorted. "After that six months, he's got three months shadowing each man. Hector, Vance, Mace, Luke and finally me. He'll learn by seeing, then doing, and he won't be involved in anything that he's not ready for. That's for him but that's also for the protection of the team. After that, he's got a year where he gets assignments I'd give Bobby or Matt. Assignments where he doesn't go out without a partner until I'm sure I can step that up and he can go out alone. That's nearly two years in training and a year of what's essentially probation before I'll even consider him taking shit on as a full-fledged member of the team."

Huh.

Well.

Shit.

"And just so this is all out there, if Sniff gets out of the armed forces and he wants a spot on my team, he knows that's guaranteed," Lee continued. "The Army will teach him most of what he'll need to know and we'll fill in any gaps. I have no questions in my mind he'll serve his country and come to me the man I'll need him to be. And when that happens, Shirleen, I'll look forward to having him on my crew."

Huh.

Well.

Shit.

"Are you done laying me out now?" Lee asked impatiently.

"You should have told me," I declared.

"It's the men we both want them to be that they wanted to do it and obviously, I agreed," he shot back.

Huh.

Fuck.

Whatever.

"Roam is an exceptionally gifted writer," I shared.

"Good. I'll look forward to reading his mission reports," Lee returned. "Now are we done?"

"You're a pain in my ass, Liam Nightingale," I told him.

"Glad that feeling is mutual. Now we're done," he muttered.

And then he hung up on me.

Slowly, I took the phone from my ear and narrowed my eyes at it.

"Baby," Moses whispered.

I raised narrowed eyes to him.

He did not, as many did (and should), rear back.

He grinned at me.

"Have I failed to tell you I was in the Army?" he asked.

He did, indeed, fail to tell me that.

"You were in the Army?" Sniff asked.

Moses turned to him. "Yeah. It's a good choice, son."

Lord!

"The vapors are comin' back," I declared.

Three sets of male eyes turned to me.

All three were amused, though two were also exasperated.

The brain behind one of those sets made a decision.

"You're on duty," Roam announced, his attention to Moses while tagging the sleeve of Sniff's shirt and pulling him toward the front door. "Her vapors are serious. Good luck," he finished.

"You're gonna need it," Sniff muttered as he followed Roam.

Moses just shook his head, smiling and watching them go.

I moved to the wide hall that led by the kitchen to the front door.

"Where you boys going?" I called.

"Out," Roam answered, but he wasn't done. He stopped at the door and turned my way. "And for the record, we're not at the place in this situation where we're down with some dude spending the night with our mom."

"Totally not down," Sniff agreed.

I felt Moses come to stand behind me as I studied the ceiling.

But one could say (that one being *me*) I absolutely *loved* the words "our mom" coming out of my boy's mouth.

The front door opened and I looked there.

"Be good. Do right. Make good decisions. And *come home safe to your mother!*" The last I shouted because the door was closing.

"Those boys," I mumbled irritably after the door shut.

I barely got that out before I was turned into Moses's body with his arms around me.

I put my hands on his biceps (as best I could with one, seeing as I still had my phone) and looked up at his face.

His eyes were roving over mine.

"Was in the room when both of my daughters were born," he shared strangely.

"Yeah?" I asked.

His gaze finally stopped on mine. "So that was the third most beautiful thing I witnessed in my life."

Oh no.

I was going to start crying again.

I swatted his arm and warned, "You're gonna make me cry."

"Have at it. All your mascara's gone already. There's no reason to hold back anymore."

Oh no!

I put my hands over my face, conking my own damned self with my phone.

Lord, I was a mess.

He shoved my face in his chest.

"Are you even partially clued in to how much those boys love you?" he whispered into the top of my 'fro.

I was.

I absolutely was.

As an answer, I took my hands from my face, wrapped my arms around him and pressed my cheek to his chest.

Boy, it felt so good being in his arms, I could just hug this man…

For eternity.

"Yeah," I whispered back.

"So if anyone ever told me I was gonna get caught by my woman's two teenage boys after making love to her for the first time, necessitating me scrambling to get my clothes on, and help her with hers, I'd take that blow if they told me I got to witness what I just saw."

I tipped my head back, mascara traces all over my cheeks and all.

"Sorry they got in your face," I said.

"I'm not," he replied.

I smiled at him.

Moses smiled back and gave me a squeeze.

"You hungry?" he asked.

I was feeling a might peckish.

I nodded.

He smiled again. "You wanna fix your face?"

Was he seriously asking that question?

I nodded again.

"Go fix your face, baby," he urged quietly, dipping his head and touching his mouth to mine. "I'll wait."

I touched my mouth to his right back.

Then I scooted out of his arms to my room to fix my face.

When I got there, my bathroom seemed different.

Like it was shiny and new.

I had a feeling I'd have to get used to that kind of strangeness all around me.

Though I wouldn't know, I'd never experienced it.

But my guess was that was how things seemed when your future was bright.

Just FYI...

I would find my guess was right.

EPILOGUE
SHE MADE ME BELIEVE

Moses

S*ome time later...*

"Hey."

Moses looked to the man walking through the side door that led into the vestibule.

"Hey, son," he replied.

Roman started toward Moses.

The tux looked good on him.

Roman shifted his trajectory, moved to the closed door to the sanctuary and looked through the windows.

"It's my understanding you and Julien are supposed to be walkin' out to stand at that altar right about now, meetin' me there," Moses observed.

Roman turned his head Moses's way and shared, "Sent a message to her. She knows I need some time."

Moses drew breath in through his nose.

It was then Roman walked to him, asking, "She been cryin' a lot?"

"Daisy's had to put her false eyelashes back on three times."

A ghost of a smile formed on his lips.

"Say what you gotta say, son, there's important shit that's gotta get done today," Moses prompted.

Roman focused on him in a way that Moses held his breath.

"Nothing will ever harm her."

His tone was utterly inflexible.

Moses's throat closed.

"And I will love and protect her and the children I'll make with your daughter until the day I die," Roman continued.

"Roam," Moses forced out.

"She means everything to me," Roman told him.

"You haven't hidden that," Moses replied.

And praise be to the Lord he had not.

Not from the beginning.

Roman examined Moses's face before he nodded and moved back to the doors to the vestibule.

He looked through the window.

"Thank you for lovin' her the way you do," he said quietly.

He was looking at his momma sitting in the front pew.

"It hasn't been hard," Moses replied in the same tone.

And that was the damned truth.

Roman turned to him.

"She made me believe in love," he shared.

Moses nodded.

"And she taught me how to do it," Roman went on.

Moses knew full well the way Shirleen loved. He'd now had years of learning how deep that woman could love.

"Then my baby girl is gonna get what she deserves."

"Yes, she is."

That was a vow.

Moses moved to him and lifted his hand to rest it on that broad shoulder.

"Son, go," he whispered. "Go on. Marry my daughter."

Roman lifted his hand and took hold of the side of Moses's neck.

After a firm squeeze, he dropped it and Moses's hand fell when Roman stepped away.

Moses watched as Roman walked back to the door that led to the side hall.

He moved through it.

The door closed.

Moses turned his attention from there to the window Roman had been looking through.

The mother of the groom was sitting in her pew on her boy's side, her head turned, leaned over the arm rest at the end of the pew, her eyes aimed through the window at her husband.

They'd had a number of discussions about where they were going to sit.

Shirleen Richardson was not to be deterred from taking her boy's side.

Since her mother was sitting on her side, his daughter was entirely down with her dad sitting beside her fiancé's momma.

"You'll get to see my face from there, Daddy. Not my back," she'd told him.

That had decided it.

He watched his wife tip her head to the side.

She had some subtle glitter in that gorgeous 'fro.

She looked beautiful.

He smiled at her.

Her pretty face got soft before she forced herself to toughen up so she wouldn't lose it (again) and she smiled back.

He watched her turn to face forward.

Only then did he step away to wait for his daughter to come to him.

It was his girl's wedding day and Moses Richardson was not jittery. He was not worried. He had no reservations.

He knew, from the beginning, that Roman Jackson would do anything to win his girl then hold her safe.

He'd even proved it.

Without a doubt.

So Moses had not a single reservation.

He loved that man like a son.

And he knew Roman would make his girl happy.

Though, through the ride that had brought them all right there, Moses could have done without the kidnappings.

The End

KristenAshley.net
NEW YORK TIMES BESTSELLING AUTHOR

Go back in time before the Rock Chicks and Hot Bunch were a thing and read the Rock Chick prequel.

Rock Chick Reawakening
the story of Daisy and Marcus.

LEARN MORE ABOUT ROCK CHICK REAWAKENING

Rock Chick Reawakening shares the tale of the devastating event that nearly broke Daisy, an event that set Marcus Sloan —one of Denver's most respected businessmen and one of the Denver underground's most feared crime bosses—into finally making his move to win the heart of the woman who stole his.

Book 8.5 of the Rock Chick Series is a novella that travels back in time to share the story of beloved character, Daisy and her honey bunches of love, Marcus.

Keep reading for an excerpt of Rock Chick Reawakening.

ROCK CHICK REAWAKENING
PROLOGUE

Building Castles
Daisy

"You're a lunatic!"

"You didn't think that when I had my mouth wrapped around your dick!"

"That's because you couldn't use it to talk!"

"Kiss my ass!"

"Not anymore, babe. We're done."

"Like I care."

"You'll care when you got no one's dick to suck to pay your cable bill."

My eyes were closed. I was lying alone in my dark room, on my back in my twin bed.

My bed was lumpy, seeing as Momma bought it from a yard sale, but I didn't feel that.

And my room was small and it didn't smell all that great, this coming mostly from the carpet. It smelled like that from all the way back when, when we first moved in. Momma didn't bother to do anything and got mad when I complained about it, so I'd tried to clean it myself, three times. But that smell just wouldn't go away.

I didn't smell the smell either.

And I could hear the words but even though they were coming from just down the hall, I was somewhere else.

I was building castles.

"Do not go there!"

"Fuck off."

"I'm tellin' you, *do not go there!*"

The door to my bedroom opened and so did my eyes, the beautiful castle I was building melting clean away.

I could smell the smell.

I could feel the lumps.

I could sense the closeness of the room, its thin walls, its fading, ripped-in-places wallpaper, the ceiling light I never turned on because the cover had been shattered on a night I didn't like to remember and now it made it too bright when I turned on the light.

"Daisy, sweetheart?" he called.

I looked to the door.

He was in shadows, those caused by the dark of my room and the hall. The only light was coming from somewhere else, probably her bedroom, because it was real late.

Tall, he had a beer belly but he also had broad shoulders.

I liked his shoulders. And his eyes. They were always twinkling when they looked at me. Even when he was mad at Momma, he'd look at me and it was like he forced the ugly out so all he'd ever give me was just the twinkle.

And he always used that soft voice when he talked to me.

Always, even when he was fighting with Momma, like just then.

"*Get away from that door!*" my mother screeched and I saw the shadowed man jolt as she shoved him to the side.

He came back, hand up, finger pointed in her face.

"Chill," he bit off.

I wanted to close my eyes but I didn't. I never could in times like these. Times like these, it was impossible to build castles. I knew this sure as certain.

Seeing as I'd tried.

His head swung back to me.

"I gotta go, girl. You need somethin', all you gotta—"

"She don't need shit!" my mother snapped.

His head turned to her again. He hesitated and I watched as his body moved when he took in a deep breath.

Then he looked back to me.

"I'm sorry, sweetheart," he whispered.

So was I.

I was young, only ten, but I understood why he was sorry.

But he wasn't sorrier than me.

"You tell *her* you're sorry. You treat me like garbage and you tell *her* you're sorry?" Momma shouted and the shadowed man jolted again because she'd shoved him again.

He reached in, grabbed the knob to my bedroom door, and pulled it to.

He did stuff like this too, a lot, because they fought, a lot. He tried to make it so I wouldn't see. Coming down the hall and closing my door. Or when they were in the middle of it and I was in the living room or kitchen, telling me quietly, "Maybe you should go to your room, sweetheart, and close that door, yeah?"

But he could never make it so I wouldn't hear.

With that, he disappeared.

But she didn't.

Her voice still came at me.

"That's it? You're just leaving?"

Nothing from him.

But more from her.

"You can't be serious. You cannot be freaking serious!"

He didn't reply.

"You're such an asshole. A total *freaking asshole*."

He wasn't an asshole.

He was a good one.

The *only* good one.

Or, at least, the only good one I'd met.

He didn't hit her. He didn't hit me. Both of these my daddy did before he took off and we never saw him again. And other ones did besides (her and me).

He didn't steal her money (Daddy did that too). He didn't look at me in a way that made my skin feel funny (it was good that Daddy didn't do *that*). He didn't eat all the food in the house and drink all Momma's beer and bourbon and then complain there was never any food or beer or bourbon in the house and ride her behind until she got in her junker car and went out to get more for him (and yeah, Daddy had done that too).

Those kinds stayed around a lot longer than this one did.

Too long.

But never that long.

They always left.

Like Daddy did.

And I never missed them.

Yes, even Daddy.

But I'd miss this one with his twinkly eyes and his soft voice and the way he called me sweetheart not like that was what I was, but that was what he had. A sweet heart.

No, there were not a lot of those kinds. Not for Momma.

Not for me.

"Stretch!" she shrieked. "*You get back here, Stretch! Get back here!*"

The front door slammed.

"*Fucking motherfucker!*" Momma screamed.

I closed my eyes.

Let myself drift away.

And I started again to build my castle.

"A Southern woman always has her table laid."

Miss Annamae was talking to me in her pretty dining room with the big dining room table all laid with the finest china, sparkling crystal, shining silver, and its big bunch of light-purply-blue hydrangeas with cream roses set in the middle.

She adjusted a napkin in its holder sitting on a plate that was sitting on a charger that was resting on a pressed linen tablecloth.

"If she's fortunate," Miss Annamae went on, and standing opposite the table to her, the fingers of my hands wrapped over the back of a tall chair, all ears, like I always was when I was with Miss Annamae, I watched her move around the table with difficulty. She wasn't a young woman. She also wasn't a beaten one, even losing both her kids and her husband and having to carry on alone. "She can change it with the seasons. I have Christmas china." Her faded blue eyes turned to me and a smile set the wrinkles in her face to shifting. "But you've seen that, haven't you, Miss Daisy?"

"Yes, ma'am."

And I had. Miss Annamae did her house up real pretty at Christmas. She always made sure I came over so she could show me all around and give me a tin of Christmas cookies she baked herself.

Momma had been working for Miss Annamae now for over two years. It was the longest job she'd ever had. She usually got fired a lot sooner than that.

I reckoned Miss Annamae kept her on as her daily girl not because she liked her or she did good work and kept a tidy house (which she did not, not Miss Annamae's and definitely not ours). I also didn't reckon she kept her on because she liked the fact Momma would be late a lot, show up hungover a lot, call off sick a lot, or one of her "men friends" would show at Miss Annamae's big, graceful mansion and cause a ruckus.

No, I didn't reckon any of this was why Miss Annamae kept her on.

I didn't know why Miss Annamae kept Momma on.

Except for the fact she was a good Southern woman.

Miss Annamae turned to the big window that faced her back garden, calling, "Come here, child."

I moved directly to her.

When I got there, she lifted her scrawny, veined hand to my shoulder and rested it there.

It felt light and warm.

"She works in her garden, a good Southern woman," she shared, her eyes still aimed out the window. "She cuts her own flowers, arranges them for her own table."

We didn't have any flowers at our house. It was actually good when the yard died during that drought last summer and became a big patch of dirt and scrub. It looked better not overgrown. Like someone lived there, they just didn't care. Instead of looking like no one lived there, and no one would ever want to.

The landlord didn't agree. He got up in Momma's face about it a lot. But she ignored him like she always ignored him when he got up in her face about things. Like the neighbors complaining about the fights or when she'd play her music too loud, which was also a lot, on all counts.

"You have sweet tea in your fridge, sugar, always," she said to me.

I nodded, looking from her colorful garden to her and feeling some pressure from her hand on my shoulder as she rested into me, giving me her weight.

I stood strong and took it. I'd take all her weight if she needed to give it to me. That's how much I liked Miss Annamae. And she had *all* my like seeing as Momma was how she was, her men were how they were, the kids at school were how they were, the teachers, the lady behind the counter at the store.

Everybody.

Yes, Miss Annamae had all my like mostly because there was no one else who'd let me give it to them.

This made it sad that Momma didn't let me come with her to Miss Annamae's house often, even though Miss Annamae always acted like she was real happy when I came. And I knew down deep in my heart this wasn't because I helped Momma and did all the gross stuff, like cleaning the toilets, so she could have a break from that kind of thing. But I did it a whole lot better than Momma did so Miss Annamae actually had the house kept the way she was paying to keep it.

Still, Momma didn't let me come often. Not even when I was in school and I had to walk home by myself and stay there by myself until she finished work (and then again stayed by myself when she went right back out).

I didn't know why this was either, except, even if it was mean to think, Momma didn't like it that Miss Annamae liked me.

I didn't understand this. If Momma was quiet and respectful, like Miss Annamae had told me a lady should be, a lot more people would like her.

I was beginning to think Momma didn't care if anyone liked her. So much, she'd rather they *didn't* like her so she didn't have to bother with people at all.

"No matter what you're in the middle of, a caller comes, you open your door to them, you invite them into your home, and you make certain they don't leave hungry," Miss Annamae carried on, taking my attention again.

Not easy to do in my house where Momma spent her money on smokes and booze and not so much on food for her kid.

I was looking forward to the day when I could get a job and I could have money and I could use it for whatever I wanted. I wasn't going to use it on smokes and booze, for certain. I wasn't going to use it on fancy dresses or shoes or handbags either.

I was going to keep my house like a good Southern woman would. My yard would be perfect. My house would be tidy. And there'd always be sweet tea and food in the fridge.

"Yes, ma'am," I said to Miss Annamae.

I felt her fingers curl on my shoulder and I was looking at her but I still felt sure as certain that her gaze grew sharper on me.

"A good Southern girl pays attention in school." She lifted her other hand to her temple then reached out and touched the middle of my forehead before she dropped it. "Ain't no call for a Southern woman to rub your nose in the fact she's smarter than you. But make no mistake, she's gonna be smarter than you."

I nodded.

She shifted closer and it felt like her eyes were burning into me.

"You find that time when you get yourself a boy, child, he holds the door for you. You enter a room before him. He closes you safe in his car. If you're at a restaurant, he gives you the seat with the best view. He stands when you stand. He offers you his hand when it's needed. And if you've got a touch with a drill and a hankerin' to use it, then you use it, girl. But if you don't and you got hooks you need put up in your bathroom, he best be gettin' on that for you and doin' it without any backtalk or delay."

"Yes, ma'am," I whispered, the wonders of such a boy as I'd never known making my insides feel funny.

"As for you, Miss Daisy, you take care of yourself," she continued. "Don't you leave the house without your hair set, your face done, and your earrings in." She patted my shoulder but then gripped again tight. "You get older, you'll find your style. And don't you let anyone tell you what that is. You're a good girl in a way I know you'll always be a good girl. Be proud of that. Good posture. Chin up. Show your pride, sugar. Be who you are however that evolves and don't let anyone cut you down."

Gosh, but it felt nice her saying I was a good girl.

It was harder to think of not letting anyone cut me down. That was always happening. I'd decided just to get used to it.

She let my shoulder go to put her hand in the pocket of the pretty, flowered dress.

She pulled out a small, dark-blue box with a white bow.

I took in a hard, quick breath.

"And last, Miss Daisy, a good Southern woman always has her pearls," she said softly.

I looked from the box to Miss Annamae, but she was blurry

seeing as I had tears in my eyes.

"Miss Annamae." My voice was croaky.

She lifted the box to me.

"Daisy, a gift is offered, you take it, you express your gratitude and later, you write a thank you note," she instructed.

I nodded, taking the box.

I pulled the bow but held it in my fist as I flipped open the top.

Inside, on a delicate gold chain, the prettiest, daintiest thing I'd ever seen, hung add-a-pearls. Their creamy gleam made me feel dazzled. The one in the middle was the biggest, getting a little bit smaller as they went down each side.

"One for every year of your life, child," Miss Annamae told me and I counted them.

She was right.

There were thirteen.

And I was thirteen.

That day.

It was my birthday.

"Now, to keep that set the way it should be, you come to me when you're fifteen and I'll add the next two pearls, balance it out," she shared.

My gaze drifted up to hers. "Miss Annamae," I repeated, my voice still sounding all choked.

And suddenly, with a swiftness I'd never seen her move, she was leaned into my face.

"You hide that from your momma. You hear Miss Annamae?"

I nodded, doing it fast.

I heard her.

Oh yes, I did.

"You wear those when the time's right. They're yours, Daisy. So you wear them when the time is right." She drew in a breath so big, I saw her draw it, before her voice got softer but no less strong. "They're yours, child. However you need them when the time comes, they're yours."

I didn't understand what she meant by that but she was being so serious I felt it best to nod, and again do it fast.

"Thank you," I whispered.

The fierce went out of her face and she cocked her head to the side. Her soft, white hair swept back in the bun filtering with the sunlight coming in her window like she was an angel, she smiled as she lifted a hand and brushed my bangs sideways on my forehead.

"Every girl needs pretty things, every girl needs a little bit of sparkle however she can get it, but every *Southern* girl needs her pearls," she whispered back.

"*Daisy!*" Momma yelled from somewhere in the house.

I jumped.

Miss Annamae closed her eyes. Her wrinkles shifted again with her frown before she opened them, looked at me and said, talking quietly, "I'm sure your momma's got good in her, girl, but just to say, a Southern woman *does not* yell."

I nodded again.

She nodded back. "Go find your momma, child."

I stepped away, took another step, and started to turn.

But I stopped and turned back.

"Miss Annamae?"

"I'm right here, Daisy."

What did I say?

No.

How did I say *all* I wanted to say?

The words got caught, twisting, filling my throat.

"*Daisy!* Where are you?" Momma shouted.

"I know," Miss Annamae said, and from the look on her face I saw by some miracle she *did* know exactly what I needed to say without me having to say it. "Now go to your momma, child."

I nodded yet again, the feeling in my throat making wet pop out in my eyes.

I swallowed, took in a big breath, dashed my hand on my eyes and shoved the box into the pocket of my jeans.

Then I turned and walked slowly out of the dining room.
Like a lady.

"I suppose you'll be wantin' some cake and ice cream or somethin'," Momma muttered when we were in her car on the way back home from Miss Annamae's house.

"No, Momma. It's okay."

"Now she's bein' that passive-aggressive bullshit," Momma kept muttering, now to herself, sort of. It was also to me.

I closed my mouth.

Momma didn't stop at the store.

In the end, I made myself bologna sandwiches for my birthday dinner while Momma got ready to go out to DuLane's Roadhouse.

But after she was gone, I ate my sandwiches sitting in front of the TV and I did it wearing pearls.

And three days later, Momma lost her job with Miss Annamae seeing as she went to work (late) and found Miss Annamae had passed quietly in the night while she was sleeping.

I walked away from Quick Swap with the cash in my pocket.

I went right to the bus station.

I bought a ticket and sat outside on the bench, my two suitcases on the sidewalk by my boots.

The bus came.

The driver tossed my beat-up, second-hand suitcases under the bus and I climbed in.

There weren't a lot of folks there, which was good. I didn't feel in a friendly mood and Miss Annamae had taught me that a lady can make a stranger a friend in no time flat…and she *should*.

I picked a seat at the back by the window.

I rested my head against it and stared out, unseeing.

I heard the bus start up and felt it pull away from the curb.

When it did, I also felt the wet drip from my eye, rolling down my cheek. Then some more from the other eye.

I let myself have that. Just for a spell. Doing it, lifting my hand and touching my fingers to my neck where the pearls I'd worn every day for the last two years no longer were.

They were at Quick Swap.

The time had come when I needed them.

I knew Miss Annamae wouldn't mind. I understood her now. I understood a lot of things. Most of it I wished I didn't.

They were gone, all I had of her. She gave them to me on my thirteenth birthday and I'd pawned them on my nineteenth.

I'd miss them.

But not as much as I missed her.

When it was time to be done crying, I made myself be done. I opened my purse with its cracked fake leather and fished out my hankie (because Southern women carried hankies). I also pulled out my compact. I dabbed my eyes and carefully, swaying with the bus's movements in order not to make a mess of it (but I'd been doing it now for some time and I was good at it), I fixed my makeup.

I returned everything to my purse, kept it tucked in my lap, and looked down the long bus out the front window.

We were headed west.

It was going to be a long journey.

I rested my head back on the seat and closed my eyes.

Passing the time as the bus rolled over the miles, I built castles.

Rock Chick Reawakening is available now.

ABOUT THE AUTHOR

Kristen Ashley is the *New York Times* bestselling author of over eighty romance novels including the *Rock Chick, Colorado Mountain, Dream Man, Chaos, Unfinished Heroes, The 'Burg, Magdalene, Fantasyland, The Three, Ghost and Reincarnation, The Rising, Dream Team* and *Honey* series along with several standalone novels. She's a hybrid author, publishing titles both independently and traditionally, her books have been translated in fourteen languages and she's sold over five million books.

Kristen's novel, *Law Man*, won the *RT Book Reviews* Reviewer's Choice Award for best Romantic Suspense, her independently published title *Hold On* was nominated for *RT Book Reviews* best Independent Contemporary Romance and her traditionally published title *Breathe* was nominated for best Contemporary Romance. Kristen's titles *Motorcycle Man, The Will*, and *Ride Steady* (which won the Reader's Choice award from *Romance Reviews*) all made the final rounds for Goodreads Choice Awards in the Romance category.

Kristen, born in Gary and raised in Brownsburg, Indiana, was a fourth-generation graduate of Purdue University. Since, she has lived in Denver, the West Country of England, and she now resides in Phoenix. She worked as a charity executive for eighteen years prior to beginning her independent publishing career. She now writes full-time.

Although romance is her genre, the prevailing themes running through all of Kristen's novels are friendship, family and a strong sisterhood. To this end, and as a way to thank her readers for their support, Kristen has created the Rock Chick Nation, a series of programs that are designed to give back to her readers and promote a strong female community.

The mission of the Rock Chick Nation is to live your best life, be true to your true self, recognize your beauty, and last but definitely not least, take your sister's back whether they're at your side as friends and family or if they're thousands of miles away and you don't know who they are.

The programs of the RC Nation include Rock Chick Rendezvous, weekends Kristen organizes full of parties and get-togethers to bring the sisterhood together, Rock Chick Recharges, evenings Kristen arranges for women who have been nominated to receive a special night, and Rock Chick Rewards, an ongoing program that raises funds for nonprofit women's organizations Kristen's readers nominate. Kristen's Rock Chick Rewards have donated hundreds of thousands of dollars to charity and this number continues to rise.

You can read more about Kristen, her titles and the Rock Chick Nation at KristenAshley.net.

facebook.com/kristenashleybooks
twitter.com/KristenAshley68
instagram.com/kristenashleybooks
pinterest.com/KristenAshleyBooks
goodreads.com/kristenashleybooks
bookbub.com/authors/kristen-ashley

ALSO BY KRISTEN ASHLEY

Rock Chick Series:

Rock Chick

Rock Chick Rescue

Rock Chick Redemption

Rock Chick Renegade

Rock Chick Revenge

Rock Chick Reckoning

Rock Chick Regret

Rock Chick Revolution

Rock Chick Reawakening

Rock Chick Reborn

The 'Burg Series:

For You

At Peace

Golden Trail

Games of the Heart

The Promise

Hold On

The Chaos Series:

Own the Wind

Fire Inside

Ride Steady

Walk Through Fire

A Christmas to Remember

Rough Ride

Wild Like the Wind

Free

Wild Fire

Wild Wind

The Colorado Mountain Series:

The Gamble

Sweet Dreams

Lady Luck

Breathe

Jagged

Kaleidoscope

Bounty

Dream Man Series:

Mystery Man

Wild Man

Law Man

Motorcycle Man

Quiet Man

Dream Team Series:

Dream Maker

Dream Chaser

Dream Bites Cookbook

Dream Spinner

Dream Keeper

The Fantasyland Series:
Wildest Dreams

The Golden Dynasty

Fantastical

Broken Dove

Midnight Soul

Gossamer in the Darkness

Ghosts and Reincarnation Series:
Sommersgate House

Lacybourne Manor

Penmort Castle

Fairytale Come Alive

Lucky Stars

The Honey Series:
The Deep End

The Farthest Edge

The Greatest Risk

The Magdalene Series:
The Will

Soaring

The Time in Between

Mathilda, SuperWitch:

Mathilda's Book of Shadows

Mathilda The Rise of the Dark Lord

Misted Pines Series

The Girl in the Mist

Moonlight and Motor Oil Series:

The Hookup

The Slow Burn

The Rising Series:

The Beginning of Everything

The Plan Commences

The Dawn of the End

The Rising

The River Rain Series:

After the Climb

After the Climb Special Edition

Chasing Serenity

Taking the Leap

Making the Match

The Three Series:

Until the Sun Falls from the Sky

With Everything I Am

Wild and Free

The Unfinished Hero Series:
Knight

Creed

Raid

Deacon

Sebring

Wild West MC Series:
Still Standing

Other Titles by Kristen Ashley:
Heaven and Hell

Play It Safe

Three Wishes

Complicated

Loose Ends

Fast Lane